D1176004

AFTER THE HOLIDAYS

AFTER THE HOLIDAYS

Yehoshua Kenaz

Translated from the Hebrew by Dalya Bilu

HARCOURT BRACE JOVANOVICH, PUBLISHERS
San Diego   New York   London

Library of Congress Cataloging-in-Publication Data
Ḳenaz, Yehoshuʻa.
  After the holydays.
    Translation of: Aḥare ha-ḥagim.
    I. Title.
PJ5054.K36A713 1987   892.4'36   86-31958
ISBN 0-15-103959-3

Designed by Francesca M. Smith

Printed in the United States of America

First United States edition

A B C D E

AFTER THE HOLIDAYS

Part One:

TRAIN STREET

· 1 ·

IT WAS EXACTLY EIGHT O'CLOCK IN THE EVENING AND THE CLOCK in the big room in Hadassah Friedman's house began to strike.

The teacher Borochov said to himself, If only that drunk Friedman doesn't turn up all of a sudden.

Hadassah's father was an alcoholic, and every night he would come home swaying on his feet from all the wine he had imbibed with the cart drivers in the colony. Most of the time, two sturdy cart drivers would carry him home while he sang his song, perhaps the only song he knew:

> A tender hand she had
> Nobody dared,
> Nobody dared to touch it. . . .

It was eight o'clock, and the teacher Borochov and Hadassah Friedman sat next to the table in the big room, facing each other. Hadassah lowered her eyes to the table, and Borochov held his hat in his hand and didn't know what to

3

say. On the wall opposite him hung a picture of Hadassah's mother, a big picture in an ornate frame. She had been dead for many years.

"Take a sweet, Mr. Borochov," said Hadassah, indicating a shallow dish of green glass, full of sour candies, which was standing next to a bowl of oranges left over from the winter.

Borochov put his hat down on the table, took a sticky candy between two careful fingers, and smiled his thank you at Hadassah.

"I hear, Miss Hadassah, that you have obtained employment, or so they say in the colony," said the teacher Borochov.

Hadassah smiled and said that the employment was only temporary. One of the women workers at the candy factory was ill, and Hadassah was taking her place until she recovered. The sour candy was from the factory. On Fridays the factory workers were allowed to take a few of these sour candies home, and they were searched on their way out to make sure that they hadn't stolen any other sweets as well.

The teacher Borochov said, "Outside the sky is full of stars, the gardens are blooming, and the smell is intoxicating."

And Hadassah said, "Yes, Mr. Borochov. The orange groves are in blossom now too, and soon the trees will shed their blossoms and there will be a new crop of Valencias and work in the packing sheds to wrap the fruit."

"I love nature," said Borochov, and took another candy from the dish.

"A glass of tea, Mr. Borochov?" inquired Hadassah.

There was a sound of footsteps at the back entrance. Hadassah's father was already drunk. Two cart drivers were supporting him on either side.

"Her lips were made to kiss, Sweet rosebuds of bli-i-ss, Oh mama, Sweet rosebuds of bliss!" roared the drunk.

The two cart drivers apologized to Hadassah and made off through the kitchen. The teacher Borochov stood up and went over to the bookcase. He took down a little booklet and began reading it. Hadassah went into the bedroom.

"Hadassah, remember your mother," wailed the old man. "Remember her always, remember how she spent all day cooking, sewing, cleaning the house, and looking after the goat. And how good she was to me."

And Hadassah replied, "Yes, Father. Go to sleep."

Borochov walked about the room. He paused in front of the big clock, took out his watch, and adjusted it.

Hadassah returned to the room and sat down. Borochov sat opposite her and took his hat in his hand. From the bedroom the sound of singing interrupted by hoarse sobs issued forth: "Oh Mama, her lips were made to kiss . . ."

Hadassah stood up, closed the door, and returned to the table. "How goes the pedagogic work, Mr. Borochov?" she inquired. "Take an orange. From last winter still. As good as new."

She took an orange from the bowl and began to peel it delicately. A long narrow ribbon of peel fell from the knife to the table. She moved her head slightly, and an admiring smile flickered in her eyes.

"Miss Hadassah, summer is upon us, stirring new feelings in our breasts. In the winter man too hibernates, but in summer he awakes" (he emphasized the word by raising his voice) "and contemplates the beauty of his fellow creatures and the world. The jackals howl in the orange groves, and on the women's training farm the girls sing Russian songs until late at night."

"On the training farm," said Hadassah, "they have planted new seeds and fertilized the trees, and the work gladdens the hearts of the girls. Their cheeks are red from the sun. They work all day long, and in the evening they read poetry and Hebrew newspapers."

After Hadassah had finished scraping the white pith off the orange with the blunt side of the blade of her knife, she split it in half and removed the white core with a pull. Borochov rose and walked about the room. He stopped in front of the silver candlesticks on the sideboard. They were crooked and decorated with engravings of roses and bunches of grapes. With his back to Hadassah, he stroked the engravings with the tips of his white fingers.

"Feelings," he said, "once they ripen, long to burst out, like the juice of the grapes at the end of summer."

Hadassah said, "Mr. Borochov, you speak like a poet."

In the next room the old man began to sing again:

> But on that night so clear,
> When the shadows drew near,
> She gave him all her heart,
> She gave him all her heart,
> Oh mama . . .

Borochov turned around and looked at Hadassah. She lowered her eyes. He took a sour candy from the green dish, sat down opposite her, and held his hat between his hands. The big clock struck once.

At nine o'clock Borochov put on his hat and left the house. Hadassah closed the windows and the shutters, although it was summer. A few minutes later the lights went off in the house. In the colony the streetlamps were lit, and from the women's training farm a soft singing rose into the night:

> A tender hand she had,
> Nobody dared,
> Nobody dared to touch it . . .

6

· 2 ·

"HAIM, PAY THE *GOY* AND GET RID OF HIM. YOU'RE NOT GOING
to stand and argue with him all night about the price," said
Bracha Weiss.

They were standing in the yard of their new house in Train
Street. Their things were still on the cart, and the Arab cart
driver refused to unload them until they had agreed on his
fare. Haim Weiss was filled with helpless rage. As if it wasn't
enough that the Arab was cheating him and he couldn't
speak to him and tell him what was what, his wife had to
make things worse with her defeatism.

Haim Weiss was a short, thin man. His face was like a
triangle set on his skull, his eyes small, but bright and full
of energy. His prominent cheekbones and broad forehead
gave him a cool, pleasant expression.

Batsheva came to her father's defense, arguing that they
couldn't let the Arabs get away with cheating them, not even
by a single penny. Her sister Riva said nothing. Haim Weiss
ground the dry red soil with his foot and kept his eyes fixed
on the cart.

"If only Langfuss the broker was here to argue with this
cart driver for me. Langfuss would have got the best of it,
there's no doubt of that."

The tall, broad figure of the teacher Borochov appeared
on the road, walking with a measured tread, his wondering,
childlike eyes lowered to the ground. He walked down Train
Street, crossed the railway tracks, and continued on the dirt
road leading to the citrus groves and the isolated house that
Weiss had bought.

"Here comes my relative, the teacher Borochov," whispered Weiss into Batsheva's ear. "He won't be any help. All

he'll do is start up a discussion with the cart driver about the principles of the Muhammadan religion."

Batsheva burst out laughing and Riva, her older sister, followed suit. Only the old lady, Bracha Weiss, looked at the man walking toward them. Her face was yellow with pain.

When Borochov reached the gate, he seemed embarrassed and his pink cheeks blushed a darker red. His face was full and delicate as a child's. His cheeks burned whenever he opened his mouth to say something.

The heat was heavy and humid, vapors rose from the earth. Weiss seized Borochov by the arm and introduced him to his wife and daughters. Borochov shook them all by the hand and asked why all their things were still on the cart, with the scowling cart driver barring the way with his body.

Bracha implored him, "Mr. Borochov, do us a favor and explain to Haim that we can't stand here waiting all night until the *goy* agrees to come down from the price we agreed on in advance."

Haim Weiss interrupted angrily, "What is she talking about? She doesn't understand that for me it's not a question of money. We can't let them cheat us. Once they start cheating us, they'll end up by robbing us of our land."

Borochov stood there in embarrassment. The cart driver too leaped into the fray and began putting his case to him.

"If only Langfuss was here, everything would be all right," sighed Weiss. "That Langfuss . . ."

Borochov recovered his composure, retired to a corner of the yard with the Arab, and started talking to him with gestures.

"I can do that myself!" cried Weiss, and the girls responded with waves of laughter.

Riva and Batsheva were still wearing the dresses they had brought with them from abroad, and they were wet with perspiration. Batsheva was in her early twenties and Riva was a few years older. They were both short like their father, with triangular faces like his, but Batsheva's eyes were blue-gray like her mother's.

Their mother sat down on a stone in the yard and sighed. Her face was sickly and her back stooped.

Weiss approached the Arab again, separated him from Borochov, and tried to talk to him with his skinny hands. The Arab was sick of the whole affair. He leaped furiously at the cart and began to throw the things violently onto the ground. Bracha began to bewail the damage to her property, but no one took any notice of her. They were all gazing in astonishment at the Arab. One after the other, the parcels and bundles were hurled to the ground, where they rolled over the bare yard and scattered in all directions.

When the cart driver had finished unloading the cart, he jumped onto his seat, cursed and spat mightily, whipped his horse, and galloped away in a great commotion.

Bracha Weiss stood up and began collecting the scattered bundles. The girls recovered from their astonishment and burst out laughing. Borochov could not understand what they were laughing about.

"What's so funny, for God's sake?" yelled Weiss, but his lips too parted unwillingly in a smile. "That's the way to treat them. Let them know who's boss around here! We can't let them get away with a penny."

The girls went on laughing, sending sly looks in Borochov's direction as they did so. He ran up to a heavy crate, grabbed hold of it, and turning to face them dragged it backward as far as the steps. Then he put it down and wiped the sweat from his face and neck with his handkerchief.

When most of the things were already inside the house, the thick figure of the broker Langfuss was seen coming down the road.

Langfuss was a short, fat man, with thick black brows that

met beneath his thick spectacles and ran from one side of his forehead to the other. In the colony they said that he was a man of parts who knew what he was talking about and understood all the latest scientific innovations. His head was beginning to go bald, but there was still no gray in his hair. A small, square, black mustache joined his nostrils to the middle of his upper lip, and the pale straw hat he wore in summer was always immaculate.

His short, fat hands were active, persuasive. The colony people said that he was a carbon copy of his father, who had died leaving him when he was still a young boy to care for his widowed mother. The young Moishe took over the business. The customers who once came to his father now came to him, and all his hopes of going to study in Jerusalem faded away until he stopped thinking of a university degree altogether and even took to mocking the follies of youth from which he had been saved by a miracle.

Langfuss stopped to wipe his spectacles, which had clouded over, and smiled at the Weisses and Borochov from a distance with a satisfied air.

"*Nu?*" he asked as he came in at the gate.

The girls immediately burst out laughing, but Langfuss did not lose his composure.

"I see that our teacher Borochov has made haste to get here before me," he said, chuckling politely.

Haim Weiss slapped his hands together to shake off the dust and wiped his brow with the back of his sleeve. His dark little face shone in the sweltering afternoon heat.

"A pity, Mr. Langfuss, that you did not get here earlier yourself," said the teacher Borochov. "We could have done with your advice and help."

"Mr. Borochov," said the broker with a wink, "business is business and family is family." He looked around him, and when the laughter did not die down he turned to Mrs. Weiss and asked, "And how is Mrs. Weiss feeling today?"

Bracha smiled weakly at him, but before she had time to thank him and reply to his question, Weiss drew Langfuss aside and the two of them whispered together for a few minutes.

After this, Langfuss immediately took his departure, but not before shaking them all by the hand, wishing them good luck, expressing the hope that they would outlive their present abode, and finer houses yet, inviting himself to drink a toast with them later, and giving the two laughing girls an enigmatic look.

After several hours the house began to look like a home. The whitewash was flaking from the walls, but this did not bother Weiss.

Bracha said to Borochov, "The girls are not themselves. They don't know what's happening to them. Everything is so new to them, you understand."

"They know very well what's happening to them," said Weiss sharply. "As for you, Bracha, you had better go and make us a glass of tea. We've earned it, I think."

"Where are the machines?" cried Bracha.

"What machines?" asked Borochov in alarm.

The girls choked with laughter. They fell onto each other's shoulders and swayed weakly.

"The paraffin rings," explained Weiss. "Where are they? You took them from the *goy* yourself."

"I did not," said Bracha.

"In the yard, don't you remember?" asked Riva, no longer laughing.

"She had the paraffin rings in her hands a moment ago, and already she doesn't know where she put them," complained Batsheva, breathing heavily.

"Where are the paraffin rings?" roared Weiss, and the whole house fell silent at the sound of his shrill voice trembling with anger. The teacher Borochov went outside and searched the yard for some time before coming back with two paraffin rings. Riva poured paraffin into them and Bracha brewed the tea in her new kitchen.

The kitchen was a narrow cubicle with sooty wooden walls, covered with fading oil paint. There was a little window in the wall next to the ceiling, overlooking the front yard. After the house was built, the kitchen had been joined to the other rooms by a corridor with a wooden floor leading to the closed porch next to the big room.

The four of them sat around the table, which had come a long way before coming to rest in this house, and sipped the hot tea, crunching the sugar cubes that Bracha offered them in a small crystal dish, and perspiring freely. Borochov began fanning his face with his hat, but the girls stared at him and burst out laughing, so he stopped and let the sweat run down his neck and plaster his clothes to his body.

"Who is this Langfuss?" asked Bracha, breaking the silence. All this time she had not taken her eyes off the teacher Borochov.

"A broker like all brokers," said the teacher. "Perhaps a little more honest and respectable than most."

"He frightens me," sighed Bracha.

"Are you starting already," said Batsheva sharply.

"I didn't say anything," said Bracha defensively. "I only said that he frightens me. His little eyes behind his spectacles made a bad impression on me. He looks as if he's searching for something."

"So don't marry him then," chorused Batsheva and Riva, and once more they burst into loud laughter.

Weiss lost patience. "Enough!" he shouted. "Haven't you got anything to do? Go and tidy the house a bit. This place needs cleaning. There's been nobody living here for a whole year."

Bracha shook her head and sighed heavily. Borochov rose to his feet and put on his hat. Weiss protested, "What's your hurry? Now we can entertain you in our own home."

"In our palace," corrected Bracha Weiss.

Her husband gave her a wrathful look. The teacher Borochov stood rooted to the spot. Then Weiss accompanied him to the gate.

"Come and see us, Borochov. Don't forget, blood is thicker than water."

The teacher Borochov did not reply. He waved his hand in farewell and retreated down the dirt road, keeping his eyes on the ground.

"A noble spirit," enthused Bracha, "a real intellectual."

"A gorgeous man," announced Batsheva, rolling her eyes exaggeratedly. Riva laughed.

"Poor wretches," said Bracha. "You don't even know what the word intellectual means. And how should you know? You never saw one in your father's house."

Now it was Weiss's turn to defend himself, to describe the mighty rivers that used to carry his family's timber from one end of the country to the other, the reverence and respect in which they were held by all the local people—but instead he chose to remain silent, thereby depriving Bracha of the opportunity to enlarge upon the generations of illustrious rabbis and sages who had glorified her own family line.

In the meantime evening fell and the new house grew small and gray. Bracha sat and sighed until they left her alone. Then she stood up and began to prepare the rooms for sleeping. Choirs of jackals wailed from the citrus groves that surrounded the house; they wailed right under the window and froze her blood. The house was baking from the heat of the day, but she trembled with cold under the blankets they piled on top of her and said that she was going to die.

The members of her household were used to such talk. Bracha said that the house was isolated and Arabs would come and murder them in their beds that very night, especially the cart driver whom they had cheated out of his rightful fare. Nor did she fancy Langfuss the broker. He and his little eyes darting around in his head as if they were looking for something. He would cheat them, rob them, and bankrupt them. They didn't even have enough money to go home. They should have put aside a sum of money right at the beginning, just to be on the safe side, so they would have had the money for their fare home at least.

"That murderer has brought me here to bury me," said Bracha.

Weiss's patience snapped. His skinny little body jerked in indignation, he waved his hands. He abused his wife until she fell silent and started sobbing softly, wiping her tears with the edge of the blanket.

The teacher Borochov reached the center of the colony. In the "labor exchange" next to Yardeni's shop, Friedman was sprawled drunk on the pavement with his cart driver friends applauding and cavorting around him. Borochov wanted to approach Friedman, raise him up and support him, and take him home to Hadassah. He was suddenly flooded by a great love for the whole world, but shame gained the upper hand. For a moment he was about to break into the circle of cart drivers, but his outstretched arm remained frozen in midair, while his heart pounded wildly until he was weak-kneed and breathless.

When the chorus began to howl, "Oh Mama, her lips were made to kiss . . . ," he picked up his heels and ran.

Yardeni's liqour shop made the whole colony smell of wine mingled with sour sweat, but Yardeni himself stood behind the counter erect and immaculate, white bearded and austere as a monk.

· 3 ·

THE WIDOW LANGFUSS POURED SPIRITS INTO THEIR GLASSES. THEY clinked glasses and Langfuss put a packet of expensive cigarettes on the table. Weiss did not help himself to a cigarette. Langfuss himself was a heavy smoker. There was always a cigarette stuck to his lower lip, and he would blow the ash onto his shirt and then shake it carefully off again, just like his father before him. At this morning hour the house was still cool. The widow Langfuss asked Weiss how they had settled down in their new house.

"I have yet to meet the man who was not satisfied with a deal he made with Langfuss," she said. "Sometimes I think that he cares for nothing but his reward in the world to come. His father was just the same."

The widow Langfuss was a tall, silver-haired woman with a proud and aristocratic air, who wore thick spectacles like her son.

Langfuss said: "Good luck to you, Mr. Weiss. This colony could do with a lot more people like you, people who have something to give it. If only you knew how many fly-by-nights arrive here without a penny in their pockets, a shirt on their backs, or a pair of hands that know how to work."

He fell silent and busied himself with the papers on his desk. Then he excused himself and went out of the room for a moment.

The old woman immediately seated herself on her son's chair and said to Weiss, "He has a mathematical brain. If only his father hadn't died he would have gone to Jerusalem and become a professor. How are your daughters, Mr. Weiss? Have they adjusted themselves to the country and the climate yet?"

Langfuss came back, put on his pale straw hat, and took

up his cane. Weiss rose unwillingly, said goodbye to the old lady, and went out with the broker. Outside the *hamsin* was already raging. Langfuss's house stood opposite the big synagogue square. It was a square house with faded red tiles on the roof. Two tall palms stood like sentries on either side of the gate.

The streets were almost empty. The *hamsin* whirled the dust around, making dull yellowish waves. The houses stood sleeping with shuttered windows behind rows of tall trees, surrounded by hedges of creepers, passionflowers, and dense stands of yellow honeysuckle and jasmine bushes.

An Arab riding on a donkey appeared at the bend in the road next to the big market, swaying slowly as he sighed and sang softly to himself and brushed the flies off his face with his whip.

The sight of the dead street struck gloom into Weiss's heart.

"When you bought the house in Train Street," said Langfuss, "I knew right away that you would buy an orange grove too, and I immediately thought of old Levin's grove right opposite your house."

"And why is he selling the grove?" asked Weiss.

"Levin owns a lot of citrus groves, and this is one of the biggest. He's selling it because he needs the money."

"I've never seen an orange grove before in my life," complained Weiss. "I understand nothing about it, and I don't even know how to begin to work it."

"Take yourself an overseer. A lot of people do it, you won't be the first."

"And is that the safest way of making a living around here?"

"You'll make a fortune, Mr. Weiss. The grove is young and well cultivated."

"In any case, land is always land," Weiss consoled himself.

"Quite right."

"Perhaps you can send me an overseer?"

"We'll see," said Langfuss.

"People say that overseers are a bunch of crooks," said Weiss, looking straight into Langfuss's little eyes.

Old man Levin was waiting for them in the marketplace, next to his donkey. Langfuss introduced them. Levin's donkey was as old as its master, who was an old man with a weather-beaten face, sparse gray hair, and broad, calloused hands. He rode along behind them on his donkey, proud, gloomy, and silent.

Levin didn't say a word all the way, but from time to time he muttered to himself obscurely in Arabic. Weiss looked at him askance and vowed to himself that he would never ride on a donkey. He thanked Langfuss silently for selling him a grove right next to his house so that he would not have to make a fool of himself by riding a donkey and looking after the beast.

Before consulting Langfuss and deciding to buy the orange grove, he had paid no attention to the expanses of dark green surrounding his new house. Now, with Langfuss walking by his side and giving him encouraging smiles and the old man riding on his donkey behind them, Weiss looked eagerly to the end of the dirt road and the cool shade of the citrus trees.

At the same time he tried to suppress his excitement and to tell Langfuss about the timber and the way it floated down the rivers, the huge forests they had leased, and his wife's aristocratic family. Langfuss did not show much interest in all this and contented himself with a few polite questions. When they arrived at Levin's grove, the old man got off his donkey, nodded at the Arab guard, opened the gate, and said, "That's it," like a person freeing himself of an oppressive burden.

Weiss went up to one of the trees and stroked the bark. "This I understand," he said, knocking the wood with his fist, "but not this," and he stroked one of the green balls hiding among the foliage with his slender fingers. Weiss scratched the ball with his fine nails and smelled the fruit. "A paradise on earth," he sighed.

Levin opened his mouth to say a few words, but the effort was too much for him and he changed his mind. Weiss wanted him to say something, but Langfuss seemed in no hurry to arouse the old man. He was busy with one of his endless calculations. Levin leaned against a tree and waited. He opened his mouth again and said all in one breath, "May all my enemies sell such young, well-cultivated orange groves."

"It's all right," said Langfuss to the startled Weiss, "he's only trying to praise his orange grove."

"No," said Levin, "manure was never spared here." He bent over one of the basins and cupped the loose soil in his hand. "What soil, look, look!" he screeched at them.

"Mr. Weiss says that he's paying everything in cash," yelled Langfuss into the old man's ear.

"Of course," said old man Levin, "all young, fine young trees. Now is the time they yield the most."

Weiss took hold of Langfuss's sleeve. "Don't say anything yet about the cash. First let him come down a little in the price."

The broker's face hardened.

Levin mumbled, "That's right, I bought the grove from your father, but there was no grove here then, only stones and thorns. I planted it all myself, with these two hands. Every row that grew old I replaced with young ones."

Weiss told Langfuss to bargain as he saw fit and promised that he would not interfere. From the gate of the grove he could see his house on the hill, low and isolated. He wondered how the girls would receive the news of the purchase of the orange grove. He would have to plant trees around the house.

Langfuss and the deaf old man negotiated heavily. Levin did not come down by a penny, and Langfuss did not seem any too eager to fight for Weiss's interests. Weiss felt abandoned, but he decided to wait and see how things developed. Langfuss shrugged and suggested that he try his hand himself. But Weiss kept silent and made up his mind that he would buy the orange grove whatever the price.

The deaf old man mounted his donkey and the gate shut behind them. Weiss felt a sudden terror. He wanted to begin work on the grove immediately, in case everything fell into neglect and was ruined. Langfuss seemed satisfied. The old man swayed on his donkey and sighed, "All my enemies should sell young orange groves for worthless money."

The broker reassured Weiss and begged him not to be alarmed by the old man's words. He promised him that he would try to find a reliable overseer right away.

Levin complained from behind them that he couldn't hear. Langfuss laughed and said, "Good morning, Levin."

Weiss smiled at the broker, squeezed his arm affectionately, and said, "I'm sure that everything will work out, Mr. Langfuss. Everything will work out fine. Why don't you drop in and have something to drink?"

Langfuss was in a hurry. Weiss turned onto the path leading to his house. Langfuss and Levin continued up the dirt road, crossed the railway tracks, and turned into Train Street. Weiss stood at the gate watching the short, fat broker talking with lively gestures to the old man on the donkey and tried to make out what they were saying. The roar of the hot wind impaired his hearing. The two men did not even turn around to see if he was still standing there.

When he went into the house he tried to suppress his excitement. "Girls," he said, "we have an orange grove. Here, not far from the house."

Bracha sighed.

THE TEACHER BOROCHOV sat in his room. All day long he had not stirred forth, except at lunch time to have something to eat in the colony. It was the long vacation. The days and nights seemed long and his room made him feel sleepy. He took a few books from the bookcase, but he couldn't read. His broad, childish face was tired and unshaven. His black curly hair was rumpled. The letters refused to obey his eyes and his will died inside him. He lay on his bed with the open book in front of him. He read the same passage over and over again and tried to concentrate. In vain. His thoughts were empty.

The landlady knocked at the door.

"Mr. Borochov," she said, "why don't you switch on the light? You're reading in the dark and ruining your eyes."

The room was indeed dark, and he had not realized it. He thanked her, apologized, blushed, and went on lying there in the dark. A light summer breeze came in the window and ruffled the curtains.

If only he were a poet. If only he could put down on paper even a fraction of what was in his heart, things that he himself could hardly understand. Perhaps he was sick. But his forehead was cool, and so were his throat and armpit. The landlady's daughter was playing the piano, but the tune did nothing to dispel his gloom.

He got up and put on the light. The streetlamps went on too. He looked outside hoping to see a friend or acquaintance. He went to the corner of the room, picked up the jar of cold water, and poured himself a glass.

He went to shave and returned refreshed to his room. He got dressed, put on his hat, and went out into the street. He didn't know where he was going but his feet knew. Ten minutes later they were standing outside Hadassah Friedman's house, which was dark and shuttered. The office of the cultural committee was shut too, and he didn't have the key. There was no work for him to do there that evening anyway.

In the center of the town, next to Yardeni's shop, the cart drivers had already gathered, but Friedman was not yet drunk.

The old man sat on a stone on the edge of the pavement paying no attention to the jokes of his friends.

"Everything is against me tonight," thought Borochov and self-pity welled up inside him and brought tears to his eyes.

He began walking down Train Street. On the other side of the railway tracks he was overcome by doubt and he slowed down, stopped, and turned back.

· 4 ·

BRACHA WEISS RECOVERED FROM HER ILLNESS AND BUSIED HER-self about the house all day long. The house was too small for its occupants and this meant a lot of extra work for her.

One evening there was a knock at the door. Nechama's Baruch was standing shyly in the doorway. Langfuss had sent him to offer his services as an overseer for Weiss's new citrus grove. Weiss let him in and asked him to sit down.

Baruch was a big, hefty fellow, his face burnt by the summer sun. His eyes were small and lashless and his nose was broad, red, and freckled. His greatest trouble was his big, broad hands. He never knew what to do with them, and for this reason he kept them in constant motion around his body, as if he were chasing away invisible flies, or pushed one of them through his frizzy hair while hiding the other in his pocket.

For some time he sat there saying nothing and waiting nervously for his host to begin the conversation. But his host sat and stared at him as if he were a creature from another world. Baruch pinched his thigh inside his pocket and regretted having listened to the broker and agreeing to come to see Weiss.

"Yes, sir," said Weiss to Baruch after a long silence.

"I'm Baruch."

"Yes."

"Nechama's Baruch."

"Very nice."

"Mr. Langfuss told me, you know . . ."

"What did Mr. Langfuss tell you?"

"Mr. Langfuss told me about this job here, I mean, to be overseer in your orange grove, that's what he said."

Weiss, who had known this from the beginning, now pretended to have suddenly seen the light. He raised his brows and said, "Aha . . ."

Just to be on the safe side, he quickly sent his daughters out of the room. Sure enough, gales of laughter issued from their room, and Weiss immediately shut the door.

Baruch began to blink. He plucked up his courage and said, "You can ask anyone you like about Nechama's Baruch and they'll tell you. I know how to work. Up to now I've been working all alone in Mirkin's grove with the Arabs, and Mr. Mirkin was satisfied with me."

"Why did you leave him and come to me?"

"To be an overseer." Baruch's little eyes lit up with a sweet smile, but he immediately realized the intention behind the question and he added hurriedly, "But even when I'm overseer I'll work. I can't live without working. I have to have something to keep these hands busy." And he spread out his two clumsy laborer's hands.

Weiss said nothing, but the mocking smile at the corners of his mouth disappeared. Suddenly he felt sad.

Baruch sensed this and he said, "To be an overseer is a great honor for me, and my mother wants it too." Then he was sorry for what he had said and for mentioning his mother. To correct the bad impression he said, "My mother is Nechama. Everybody knows her here in the colony."

This only made matters worse. Baruch's feet urged him to get up and run away.

But Weiss had decided to take him on. In the first place, he realized that Baruch was too slow-witted to cheat him, and overseers, he had heard, were notorious crooks. Also, he liked the idea of an overseer who would work along with the Arabs too.

"Tell me, Nechama's Baruch, do you know how to plant a tree?"

"Yes, of course, Mr. Weiss."

"Will you come tomorrow morning and plant some trees here in the yard?"

"Guavas? Everyone is planting guavas now."

"Plant whatever is customary. I rely on you."

"Today, Mr. Weiss, everybody is pulling up their old trees and planting guavas. I don't know why."

"Plant whatever you like."

"But I'll plant whatever you like, Mr. Weiss. Give me some money to buy saplings at the women's training farm, and tomorrow morning I'll plant them here in the yard."

"And plant cypresses and flowers all around, you know."

"Yes, Mr. Weiss. And about that job . . ."

"What job?" asked Weiss.

"Mr. Weiss, the job in the grove that Mr. Langfuss sent me about."

"I'll think it over and tell you tomorrow. As for wages— I hope you don't expect too much."

"No, Mr. Weiss. I support my mother, and one day maybe I'll get married too. I have to put something aside, she says. I've already built a house."

Baruch went outside and tripped over a stone in the dark yard. He cursed, stammered an apology, and hurried home.

That Langfuss knows what he's doing, thought Weiss. Up to now everything's gone smoothly. There's no reason why he should want to cheat me now.

The girls came into the room wreathed in smiles.

"That's the new overseer of our orange grove," said Weiss. "From now on see that you behave yourselves with him. Langfuss sent him, and that Langfuss knows what he's doing."

"Langfuss knows exactly what he's doing," agreed Bracha. "He wants to ruin us, I don't know why."

"Tell me, Mother," said Batsheva, "have you had one good word to say about anything since we arrived here? Is there one single thing that satisfies you in this house, in this country?"

"That murderer brought me here to bury me," replied Bracha, nodding toward her husband.

Weiss left the room. He placed a table on the closed-in porch, covered it with papers and notebooks, and sat there until late making calculations. As he did so he became conscious of the fact that his hands were slender and his fingers soft and feminine. But Bracha had called them a murderer's hands. Perhaps he had made a mistake in buying a house outside the colony. Bracha could have met other women, chatted with her neighbors, and nagged him less. The girls too sat at home alone and never met anyone, only the enigmatic Langfuss and the teacher Borochov—whom they made fun of whenever they met him without even knowing why.

The girls suddenly started singing, a Sabbath song they had sung at home when they were children. Today was Thursday. What had suddenly made them think of that Sabbath song?

The song had a gentle, dragging rhythm, and Bracha's hoarse voice too joined in with an irritating hum. As a young woman his wife had had a sweet singing voice. Weiss was suddenly overcome by weakness. The papers slipped out of his hands. His eyes misted over and he felt an urgent need to do something, but he didn't know what. The girls were singing in two voices. They had nothing to do, poor girls.

Sitting at home on a Thursday evening and singing Sabbath songs. Everything seemed strange to him here. What whirlwind had cast up him and his family in this place?

The heat was oppressive, and the fact that the porch was enclosed didn't keep the insects from swarming on the walls and around the lamp. Moths, beetles, crickets, flying ants.

He got up, took off a slipper, and began banging it frantically against the walls. The singing stopped and Riva came running to the porch.

"Carry on singing, Riva, carry on. I didn't mean to stop you. But these insects are swarming all over the place."

Riva said nothing.

"Something has to be done about them," added Weiss.

Riva went back to her room. The singing was not resumed. The house was silent again, and the vacuum was filled by the croaking of the frogs outside. Bracha sighed and said something about the Arab murderers prowling in the orange groves and around the house.

Why didn't they go on singing? Weiss would have liked Batsheva to come and sit beside him on the porch while he was busy with his accounts. She could sit next to him and knit or read a novel. It was cooler here than in the rest of the house. Bracha had made up their beds in the big room, and the girls had already gone to bed in their room.

"Much blame is due to drink, much to laughter, much to childhood, and much to evil neighbors . . ." He remembered this verse without knowing where it came from or what it had to do with anything. His eyes closed with exhaustion. He collected his papers from the table, switched off the light, and went into the big room.

Bracha was snoring in her bed, a sign that she was better and sleeping soundly. The body could recover, but her melancholy would never pass. A soft breeze stole in through the windows. He pulled the sheet up over his wife's shoulders.

She mumbled obscurely and turned over. The sheet slipped down again. He let it be and retired to his bed, where he fell immediately into a deep sleep.

THEY WOKE AT DAWN to the sound of blows and thuds in the yard. Bracha sat up in bed, pale, and muttered, "The Arabs!"

Weiss cautiously opened the shutter next to his bed and the room was flooded with the first rays of the sun. Baruch was standing in the yard and digging energetically with his hoe. When he saw the window opening he stood up straight and blinked at the sun.

"What's the time, Baruch?" asked Weiss in angry astonishment.

"About five o'clock, Mr. Weiss," said Baruch. "I'm digging holes for those trees you said about last night."

The saplings were standing ready in rusty tins in the corners of the yard.

"Waking people up in the middle of the night, wild animal," said Bracha.

"Is this the time to start work, Baruch, before dawn?"

"Yes, Mr. Weiss, that's how I always work. In the morning you have more strength because it's not hot yet."

"Come in afterward and have a cup of coffee with us."

"Thank you very much, Mr. Weiss, but I've already had my coffee this morning. Perhaps a glass of cold water."

He was in high spirits. He broke into a merry song and the hoe danced between his hands, cleaving through the dry red soil as easily as if it were butter. Weiss stood at the window unable to take his eyes off the sight. Baruch filled with pride and increased his tempo. The holes gaped beneath the blows of his hoe; he rounded the edges, raked out the stones, and pulled up the couch grass with astonishing dexterity.

"Good morning, Baruch," said Weiss suddenly.

26

"Good morning," replied Baruch without pausing in his work.

· 5 ·

HADASSAH FRIEDMAN WAS HER DRUNKEN FATHER'S ONLY daughter. Her mother had died many years before, and Hadassah hardly remembered her. She had no steady employment; in winter she went out to working wrapping fruit in the colony's packing sheds, and in the summer she stayed home, except when a special opportunity offered itself. Nobody knew what Friedman the drunk and his daughter lived on. The old man wasted his money night after night at Yardeni's shop and Hadassah did not protest.

Hadassah Friedman was a slender girl with straight black hair cropped close to her neck. Her eyes were black and burning and her lashes heavy. Friedman the drunk and his daughter's house was surrounded by tall cypresses and there was a pretty garden in the front yard. Jasmine climbed up to the low windows, and the green shutters, always freshly painted, closed early every evening, even in summer.

Hadassah had one friend, Masha, little Napoleon's sister. Masha had a very bad name in the colony, but Hadassah didn't care because Masha was a good girl. Masha had a steady job at the candy factory. She was very tall and thin, and her brightly colored dresses hung gracelessly on her narrow, prominent bones. Her hair was cut very short, her nose was sharp, and her arms were long. Her father was unemployed and their house was full of children both big and small. They lived in an old packing shed to the east of the colony; her mother worked as a chicken plucker in the abattoir in the big market.

On Saturday nights Hadassah Friedman and her friend Masha would go to the cultural committee hut, where they would sit silently on the edge of a long bench while Masha kept looking around restlessly out of the corners of her eyes. Hadassah did not know what the trouble with Masha could be and why she went to the cultural committee meetings every Saturday night without paying any attention at all to what was said. And why did she always make her come along?

The teacher Borochov stepped onto the little wooden platform and Hadassah blushed. Borochov's hand smoothed his unruly curls and his big dark lashes cast a dreamy shadow over his broad, childish face. Hadassah was unable to take in his words, but his gentle tone, his soft clear voice, and his polished pronunciation caressed the back of her neck like waves. With one hand stroking his curly hair and the back of his neck, the other drew question marks and solemn warnings in the air.

After the teacher Borochov had finished his speech, everyone rose to their feet and applauded. Slogans were shouted about Hebrew labor, and Borochov blushed with excitement and happiness, stepped down from the little platform, climbed up again, sipped a little tea that was still left in his glass on the table, and stepped down once more with a stern expression.

The audience went on shouting about labor and farmers and Arabs. Hadassah turned this way and that and suddenly she saw that Masha's place beside her was empty. She looked about her in alarm and caught sight of her friend standing in the corner of the hall in the middle of a crowd of boys who were joking with her and pinching her skinny shoulders.

Hadassah was ashamed, but she repeated to herself that Masha was a good girl.

In the meantime the teacher Borochov was coming toward her, still breathing heavily with the excitement of his speech. The bench on which Hadassah was sitting was empty. One of the boys took up a harmonica and began to play, but hardly anyone took any notice. They were all busy talking and arguing in the corners of the hall. Borochov sat down next to her, after asking her permission, to which she responded with a nod and a smile.

The teacher Borochov said, "I've never seen you at the meetings of the cultural committee before."

Hadassah said, "I come here every Saturday night with my friend Masha."

Her low voice was drowned by the noise of the harmonica. Borochov said again, pensively, "I've never seen you here before."

"Mr. Borochov," said Hadassah, "the way you spoke this evening was quite exceptional."

"Thank you, Hadassah," said Borochov. "We all do our best."

He fell silent, looked at her for a moment, and said, "It's stuffy in here, and the noise is deafening. I can hardly hear myself speak."

Hadassah clasped her hands together and then spread them out as if to ask: What can one do? Out of the corner of her eye she saw Masha laughing, shrieking with enjoyment. Her brightly colored dress stood out among the boys' white Sabbath shirts.

The teacher Borochov said, "It's cool outside now. The nights of *Tammuz*."

He rose to his feet. People had begun dancing to the strains of the harmonica, and a strong smell of dust and sweat filled the hall. Hadassah too rose to her feet. He went out before her and waited for her outside. It was a clear, fine night.

Summer nights are fine . . .
Summer nights are divine . . .
The stars are so bright,
The moon is so white,
On a summer's night . . .

sang the teacher Borochov under his breath, and smiled at Hadassah in embarrassment.

"Mr. Borochov," said Hadassah, "we left Masha inside. She must be looking for us."

Outside Mirkin's handsome house in Founders Street they stopped, and Borochov whispered, "Hadassah, Hadassah Friedman!" She was surprised to hear a note she had never heard before in his voice.

Sweet, intoxicating scents rose from the ornamental trees and the flower beds in the large garden. Borochov remembered the jasmine bushes next to Hadassah's window and his heart contracted.

"Hadassah, Hadassah . . . I've never seen you at the cultural committee on Saturday nights. I've never once seen you there. Why haven't I ever seen you?"

They went on walking up the wide street which climbed all the way to the water tower hill. The houses in Founders Street were tastefully set in flower beds, and there were avenues of palm trees planted on both sides of the street. A cool breeze was blowing on the hill by the water tower, and Hadassah was wearing a light summer dress with short sleeves.

"How are your relations, Mr. Borochov?" she asked.

"Yedidya, please call me Yedidya, Hadassah."

He stretched out his hand and stroked her smooth, delicate hand with his fingers. Hadassah said, "It's getting late, Mr. Yedidya, and my father is all alone at home. He must be worried."

But instead of going home they climbed down the hill and

entered the expanse of sand next to the Yemenite quarter. The wind ruffled Hadassah's straight black hair and lifted the skirt of her dress. They stopped next to a solitary tree. Hadassah leaned against the trunk of the old fig tree and held her skirt down with her hands to stop it from blowing up over her knees.

The teacher Borochov embraced Hadassah, clasped her to his chest, and kissed her on the lips. Hadassah dropped the skirt of her dress, lifted her arms, and embraced him awkwardly, without managing to encircle his broad body.

A donkey brayed in the Yemenite quarter and the sound echoed over the flat, empty plain. Borochov's upper lip quivered in excitement and his voice sounded like a sob.

"Good, kind Hadassah," he whispered in her ear. "Hadassah, my sweet, simple Hadassah . . ."

"You talk like a child, Mr. Borochov," said Hadassah, stroking his soft, warm throat and the chest exposed by his open shirt, which was also smooth and warm.

Borochov whispered, "It's not late yet, Hadassah. It's Saturday night, after all." And Hadassah said, "My father's alone at home. He can't make his bed up by himself."

Again they kissed, for a long time, and Borochov said many silly things to Hadassah. She laughed softly and stroked his curls. Hadassah's laughter was the loveliest and most musical sound the teacher Borochov had ever heard.

ARM IN ARM they climbed back to the water tower. There they found Masha standing in the middle of a group of boys from the cultural committee meeting, and Hadassah felt a great shame. But Masha and her friends did not notice them. Hadassah immediately averted her face, and Borochov was afraid that she was trying to get away from him. They turned around and retraced their steps through the Yemenite quarter. The full pale moon accompanied them all the way. High-pitched Sabbath songs rose tremulously from the little houses, and the smell of mint mingled with the vestiges of smoke from the outdoor ovens.

Hadassah said, "How are your two cousins settling down?"

Without his hat on, the teacher Borochov was better looking, but Hadassah did not dare to tell him so.

Borochov said, "They'll get rich, they'll work at night, buy more citrus groves, and make a fortune. In Europe too they were very rich. I don't know why they came here. They don't seem too pleased to be here."

Hadassah said, "Langfuss is telling everyone in the colony that your uncle is a wonderful man, full of energy."

"When Langfuss puts his oar in . . ." said the teacher without finishing his sentence, and embraced Hadassah again. He knew that people were talking about the strange family secluding themselves in their isolated little house outside the colony. Langfuss must be only too happy to tell everyone he met about everything that went on there. About the girls too—their silly laughter and peculiar behavior. Why should he miss such a heaven-sent opportunity? "Have you heard about the teacher Borochov's new relations?" In his mind's eye, he could see the old farmers whispering gleefully and staring inquisitively at the sickly mother and her two daughters when they came to do their shopping in the marketplace. "Like a Jewish village in the Diaspora," reflected Borochov. At the cultural committee meetings people looked at him mockingly when he made poetic, impassioned speeches about the conquest of labor, and his uncle was just like all the rest of them.

But in the meantime he had sweet, good Hadassah in his arms, and his heart was full of a different poetry. The silent, the submissive, the fragrant Hadassah. Her white dress dancing above her knees in the night breeze, her smooth black hair, and the miracle of her glowing eyes overshadowed everything else.

"Perhaps he has already made up his own bed, Hadassah," said Borochov.

They stood in front of her house. The street was deserted and the lights were out.

"No," said Hadassah, "he must have fallen asleep in his chair."

He hugged her so tightly that he was afraid of hurting her. Her voice was meek and hesitant, her eyes shy, and her hands desperately clung to the hem of her white dress.

The moon had already set, and he had no idea what the time was. His hand refused to obey him and take his watch out of his pocket.

Hadassah was tired and she didn't know what to say. She had never come home so late before. Masha was a good girl, she promised him, and her father had fallen asleep in his chair. She had to make up his bed. If he slept on the chair all night, he would wake up with a twisted neck. But in the meantime she did not go into the house. And he did not urge her to.

· 6 ·

BRACHA WEISS HAD TAKEN TO HER BED AGAIN. WAS IT SERIOUS this time? Her family thought not. Bracha called out that she was dying. But she had made this claim many times before.

Batsheva said that the resurrection of the dead took place in their house once a fortnight. Once again the cold had Bracha Weiss in its grip, and they piled all the blankets in the house on top of her. The house was closed and shuttered and sweltering.

"I'm cold," moaned Bracha.

"Yes, Brachaleh," Weiss leaned over her, "they're dragging the frozen bodies over the snow outside."

"What will you do here without me when I'm dead?" asked Bracha Weiss, and her eyes filled with tears.

Weiss lost his temper. "That's enough, Bracha, enough of that kind of talk. You're ill. All right. Rest and don't upset yourself. And for God's sake, stop moaning. We're only flesh and blood too, you know."

Bracha was silent. Weiss thought that she complained on purpose to make them all feel sorry for her.

Bracha looked well enough. But she ate nothing at all and suffered agonies of cold in the stifling room. Riva looked after her and brought her one glass of tea after the other. The kettle stood on the paraffin ring all day and all night.

Bracha asked them to fetch a doctor.

"Brachaleh," said Weiss. "You know yourself that you're not really sick. It's your nerves. Melancholia and fear of being murdered."

"Are you trying to say that I'm mad?"

"God forbid," said Weiss.

"My heart's beating too fast and I can't feel my limbs," complained Bracha.

Weiss paced nervously up and down the room but he refused to fetch a doctor.

"For your orange groves you've got the money, Haim," said Bracha.

"My orange groves?" screamed Haim Weiss. "Mine? And are the girls my daughters? Haven't you got anything to do with them? And if they find husbands and they have a bit of property of their own after we die, is that bad? Do you begrudge them their happiness?"

Riva asked them to stop quarreling.

"It's not a question of money, Riva. I'm simply ashamed to call a doctor. Explain to her, Riva, explain to her that medicines won't help her. Her illness is a mental illness. An evil spirit has taken possession of her. That's all we need, for the whole colony to find out."

"What hurts you, Mother?" asked Riva.

"I told you, my heart's beating too fast, and I'm cold. Put your hand on me, Riva, and feel for yourself."

Riva could not bear to touch her. "I believe you, Mother, but what can we do? No medicine will help you. Pull yourself together, and it will pass."

"It won't pass," said Bracha. "I'll pass. I'll pass away from this world and your father will be glad."

She began to cry again. Batsheva stood in the room and said nothing. Riva sat on her mother's bed and tried to soothe her.

"May all my enemies die before they marry their daughters," wept Bracha.

"What's she on about now," said Weiss. "She wants to drive us crazy too with her ideas."

Bracha took Riva's hand and held onto it with all her strength. Riva tried to free her hand without offending her mother.

"What will become of you, Riva?" asked Bracha. "If you listen to him, you'll remain old maids for the rest of your lives. Make friends with the teacher Borochov, Riva, he's the man for you. Do your mother a favor, Riva." She clung to her daughter's hand.

"Look at the matches your mother wants to make for you!" sniggered Weiss. "Wonderful matches! The teacher Borochov. A fat loafer, a parasite with a big mouth and a woman's hands. The woman is mentally ill, I told you so."

Riva said, "But I'm not looking for a husband now."

"No," said Weiss. "She's only saying it to annoy me. I know she is, she saw that I can't stand him and that's why she's encouraging you to make friends with that lazy liar. She's pretending to be dying to blackmail you. Brachaleh, you're not very choosy when it comes to husbands for your daughter! He makes speeches to the workers in the colony, incites them against the farmers, rants about labor—and he's never held a hoe in his hands in his life! All the farmers avoid me because of him. Look at his hands, at his white fingers. Disgusting! It's enough to make you sick."

"He'll treat you like a princess, Riva," said Bracha, taking no notice of her husband. "I know how to size people up. Don't you listen to that murderer. He wants to ruin us."

Bracha closed her eyes and let her head fall back onto the pillow. "I can feel it. This time it's serious. Sit next to me, Riva, and don't leave me alone with them. I'm afraid of them. They want to destroy us. That's why he brought us here, to kill us slowly, in agony."

"The woman's insane," said Batsheva. "She should be put away."

"Go to bed," said Weiss. "It's late. I'll look after her."

Riva and Batsheva went to their room. They made up their beds in silence, until Batsheva said to Riva in a whisper, "I hope you don't intend following her advice. He's not the man for you, Riva, that fat Borochov."

"I told you I wasn't looking for a husband."

"He's an absolute idiot, that Borochov."

Riva looked at her inquiringly.

"His head's in the clouds," continued Batsheva. "And what is our father buying orange groves for? For him? So that Borochov can waste all the money on his workers and bankrupt us?"

"There's nothing to talk about, Batsheva. The whole thing is fantastic."

"It seemed to me that you rather fancied the idea. Don't listen to Mother, she doesn't know what she's talking about."

"We should have called a doctor," said Riva.

"You can see for yourself that there's nothing wrong with

her physically. It's all in her mind, a sick desire to waste Father's money."

"Her body is as cold as ice."

"Because of her nerves," said Batsheva.

"Poor woman."

"And Father?"

"I feel sorry for them both. I feel sorry for all of us. I want to go to sleep now. Goodnight."

"Don't go to sleep, Riva," said Batsheva.

"Why not?"

"Perhaps tonight she'll really die!"

"Why on earth should she?"

"Who knows?"

"Let me go to sleep now. You can stay awake if you like and keep watch."

Riva turned her back to her sister, but she could not fall asleep. Batsheva had infected her with her fears. They did not speak but they both kept their ears open, straining to hear the sick woman's groans in the stillness. Their father did not sleep either. They heard the springs of his bed creaking underneath him. The house was dark, and they lay with their eyes open waiting for whatever would happen. Every now and then Bracha groaned and lamented her impending death, and both girls breathed a sigh of relief at the sound of the living voice.

Batsheva was sorry they had not left a light on in the house. She could hear her father awake in the next room and her heart filled with pity and sorrow. It was hot in the house with all the windows closed, and she threw her sheet off. Through the window nothing was visible in the darkness. She opened the window and a chorus of nocturnal voices pierced her ears like a continuous, deafening whistle.

Again someone turned over in bed in the next room. Her mother or her father? Would the end really come tonight?

This time there was something frightening in the air of the house. A hidden presence, mysterious and ominous.

Weiss regretted the quarrel about the teacher Borochov. Why had he lost his temper? In any case there was nothing in it. Langfuss too, he had been told, wanted to study in Jerusalem in his youth, until he settled down and applied himself to something substantial. It was his duty to be friendly to Borochov, to welcome him as a member of the family. He looked at Bracha and he couldn't hear her breathe. Now he was sorry he had not called a doctor. He was afraid to get up and approach her bed in case she was still alive. He strained his ears to hear if there was any sound from her bed. She sighed in her sleep, and he realized that he never did what he really wanted to do, but vacillated and temporized for fear of his daughters' reactions.

The way Bracha spoke made his blood boil, and he didn't know what he was saying or doing. Once they had loved each other, but it didn't last long—until Batsheva was born and Bracha was weakened by the difficult birth. She began taking to her bed at frequent intervals, and melancholy began to eat her away. The girls grew up, and from time to time her spirits would revive and she would become good tempered and submissive again, gentle as in the days of her youth. Then they would go for walks together on the riverbanks in that green landscape.

But from the day they arrived here, she had grown gloomier and gloomier. Weiss knew that if not tonight then soon, very soon, she would collapse. Or perhaps she would outlive him? This was the most terrible thing he could imagine.

The girls in their room too had not fallen asleep. He could hear Batsheva's suppressed sighs and the sound of their beds creaking. They were all waiting in suspense for morning. Bracha moaned weakly again. Was this the end? She hadn't asked for a glass of tea or gone to the lavatory for hours.

But she was still alive. Now he could hear her shallow breathing. Faint and hoarse, but breathing nevertheless.

Before dawn he saw that Bracha was sleeping soundly and he breathed a sigh of relief. Then she got up to go to the lavatory and he quickly closed his eyes so that she wouldn't see him awake and anxious. He thought that she was looking at him, and despite himself he blinked his eyes under their lids.

In the morning Bracha ate the food they brought her on a tray with a hearty appetite.

"Girls," said Weiss, "the miracle of the resurrection of the dead has taken place in our house again. We must thank the Lord for his wonders and miracles."

The girls tried to laugh.

Bracha claimed that this time she had seen death with her own eyes, but she had battled with him and defeated him, because she had made her father and mother swear that they would come to her help and intervene for her, until she saw her daughters married.

"Just as I said," said Weiss, "a miracle."

· 7 ·

ONE TUESDAY AT THE END OF THE MONTH OF *ELUL*, HADASSAH Friedman was married. The ceremony took place in the garden of the Friedman home in the afternoon, and in the evening a reception was held.

At noon Friedman the drunk and a few of his cart driver friends dragged benches and tables from the nearby synagogue and set them up on the lawn. Hadassah brought pure white sheets and covered the tables. In the middle of each table she placed a glass jar with roses, carnations, and asparagus ferns. For a week before the wedding Hadassah was busy baking and making candies, her Aunt Chasida helping her. This aunt, her dead mother's sister, was a widow who lived alone in Jerusalem.

In the afternoon Friedman the drunk bathed and had his hair cut. He put on clean white clothes. During the entire ceremony he stood quiet and obedient and did what the rabbi told him to. From time to time he stared at Hadassah and the teacher Borochov standing opposite him with dreamy, otherworldly expressions on their faces. Children stood outside the fence and gazed longingly at the bride and groom and the tables set with bowls of grapes and peanuts among the cakes and the drinks, all untouched.

Bracha Weiss stood there crying softly. Weiss and the two girls asked her to stop, but she took no notice and they were ashamed of her in front of all the people.

After the ceremony Masha, Hadassah's friend, went up to the bride and kissed her on both cheeks. "Hadassah," she said, "I wish you luck. I hope that you'll be happy all your life long and that you won't forget me."

Hadassah's eyes were wet as she embraced her friend and whispered in her ear, "It will be your turn soon!"

After Masha came Masha's mother and little Napoleon and the pale, unemployed father and all their brood of children. They all surrounded Hadassah and gazed at her in wonder as if she were a fairytale princess.

The Weiss family surrounded the teacher Borochov and shook him by the hand. Bracha held his hand in hers and shook it speechlessly up and down, nodding her head as if she were saying, "Yes . . . yes . . ."

The teacher Borochov smiled gratefully at his relations. Hadassah was dressed in white. A thin veil covered her face and lent her an air of pallor. Masha was wearing a loud dress that drew attention to her height and her prominent, masculine bones. Masha's mother whispered to her, "*Nu*, when will it be your turn, you bad girl?"

Masha said nothing but gazed at the teacher Borochov sitting silently next to Hadassah at the head of the table with a new hat on his head. Masha stared at Borochov, while her mother thought to herself that nothing had come of all the boys Masha went around with in the colony. Nothing, or perhaps worse than nothing. Because Masha had a flat chest.

Aunt Chasida invited all the guests to be seated at the tables and began to supervise the serving of the refreshments. The two musicians took up their places next to the bride and groom and broke into a merry song from the Diaspora:

"*Mazeltov, mazeltov! Mazeltov* to the groom, *mazeltov* to the bride, *mazeltov* to every Jew! Let all the *goyim* see, let them burst with envy!"

The violinist was tall, thin, and bespectacled. He closed his eyes when he played, raising his thin eyebrows and wrinkling his brow, and swayed in time to the music.

Next to him sat the drummer, who had a squint and a watering eye. He smiled as he showed off his virtuosity. He took an empty bottle in one hand and holding the two drumsticks in the other he beat the bottle with great rapidity until it sounded like a long peal of bells, or the high, merry whistle of a flute. When the violinist played a riding song, the drummer muffled his drum with one hand and with the fingers of the other he beat the sound of horses' hooves galloping and fading away into the distance.

In the beginning no one dared to join in and sing along with the artists, but gradually a hesitant voice rose in the air, eager to set out with the horsemen and waiting for companions to join him, until Hadassah's garden was loud with the sound of singing, and even Haim Weiss joined in enthusiastically, to the great embarrassment of his daughters.

The drummer threw his drumsticks in the air, caught them

in midair, and brought them down on the drum without missing a beat. He clashed the cymbals with a crash that startled all the guests from their seats. He winked at everyone with his squinting eye and demanded more and more to drink.

Only the violinist stood in his corner as if untouched by all the commotion. His fingers vibrated on the strings and his body bent over with every draw of his bow. He shook his head, swayed his shoulders, and sunk his chin into his violin as if he wanted to hide away inside it and disappear.

The Weiss family sat by themselves next to the teacher Borochov, and nobody came up to talk to them or ask them how they were. The two girls whispered to each other, pointed at various people, and giggled into their hands.

The guests began to drink, crack nuts, and eat grapes and cakes. The bride and groom, who had eaten nothing all day, were given chicken soup with rice and chicken meat to break their fast.

Hadassah's father sat next to the bride and said nothing. The cart drivers sitting next to him began to poke him in the ribs with their elbows and ask with a wink or a mumble, "*Nu*, Friedman? This isn't a funeral! We're thirsty."

Friedman looked fearfully at Hadassah, Borochov, and Aunt Chasida, who was circulating among the guests but keeping a suspicious eye on him all the time. Suddenly they saw that he had come to a decision. He took a bottle of brandy standing in the middle of the table, for decoration more than use, a large sealed bottle, pulled out the cork and filled his own glass and those of his friends. Hadassah was horrified, the guests were startled and held their breath.

The children behind the fence said, "Soon he'll be drunk and then we'll see some fun."

Aunt Chasida rushed up to the table and put out her hand to grab the bottle. But Friedman hung on to it, hugged it to his chest, smacked Chasida on the hand, and shouted, "Go away, thief! And don't poke your nose into other people's affairs!"

A silence fell on the guests. The musicians went on playing distractedly, staring nervously at Friedman. The teacher Borochov rose to his feet and approached his father-in-law, but Friedman took no notice of him. He and the cart drivers surrounding him drank bottle after bottle, sang bawdy songs, and shocked everyone with their loud laughter. Borochov signaled to the now silent musicians to go on playing, but Friedman yelled at them to stop and waved an empty bottle threateningly in the air.

Riva and Batsheva Weiss laughed loudly and shamelessly. Their mother rebuked them and begged them to show some consideration for the groom. Weiss was about to get up and teach the drunk and his friends a lesson, but Borochov stopped him.

Hadassah sat pale-faced at the head of the table, and the teacher Borochov stroked her hand gently. He said to her, "Don't be sad, Hadassah, he'll calm down soon."

Napoleon's mother sent him and all his brothers and sisters from the garden to stand behind the fence, because they were laughing out loud in front of the bride and groom.

Weiss made up his mind and approached Friedman.

When the drunk saw him coming, he welcomed him with open arms and tried to kiss him. Weiss evaded his embrace but the drunk tottered after him, saying that he refused to forgo the pleasure and the honor.

"Mr. Weiss," cried Friedman, "you are the only relation of our honored groom, standing in for his father at this wedding. You can see that I myself have had a drop to drink in honor of the wedding, believe me, only in honor of the wedding, everyone here is my witness that all year long I'm as sober as a judge!"

Friedman guffawed loudly after delivering himself of this jest. "And now, the father of the bride and the father of the groom must kiss, like our fathers before us always did at weddings."

Bracha Weiss said, "Haim, leave him alone and come back here. You're only making things worse."

But Haim Weiss refused to give up. He saw himself as the defender of the honor of the groom's family. He wanted to rebuke Friedman and send him away in disgrace, but he didn't know how. All the guests were watching him expectantly. Friedman complained that the father of the groom thought he was too good to kiss him just because he had once been a cart driver. He turned his attention from Weiss to the teacher Borochov.

"Mr. Borochov," he roared. "Drink a toast to our health! You've married a wonderful woman today, there's nobody to touch my Hadassah! She's like her mother, God rest her soul. A little on the delicate side, but a good housekeeper. Not so well educated perhaps but clever and kindhearted. Don't think I'm just a retired cart driver. We come from a good family! Drink, Borochov, drink to the health of our good family!"

"Yes, let him drink!" shouted the cart drivers.

Friedman suddenly decided to sing "A Tender Hand." He opened his mouth, flung out his hand, cleared his throat, cried "Oh . . . ," and stopped.

The silence continued in the garden, and all the guests were ashamed to look one another in the eye. Riva and Batsheva folded their arms on the table, hid their faces, and shook with laughter. The bride and groom sat with lowered eyes. Aunt Chasida retired to a corner and wept softly. She was wearing a long black dress, and her little amber earrings drew attention to the tiny ears peeping out under her neatly combed brown wig.

Friedman caught sight of Chasida and he shouted at her, "Why are you crying, Chasidaleh? You never had a husband like my Hadassah. Your husband was never as handsome and well educated as the teacher Borochov. The number of books he reads in one day you never saw in your wildest dreams. His whole belly is stuffed with them. He knows them by heart. And how he speaks Hebrew! Why are you crying, Chasidaleh? It's a wedding today and you should be happy!"

Friedman swept the plates and glasses and empty bottles away and began banging on the table with his fists and singing loudly, "I saw her when she went, when she went to draw water from the well . . ."

And all the cart drivers chorused the refrain:

> Heigh ho, from the well . . .
> I kissed her when she went,
> went to draw water from the well.
> Heigh ho, from the well . . .

Gradually the guests began to slip away from Hadassah's wedding reception. Weiss did not want to go. His wife didn't know whether this was due to stubborn family pride or curiosity about what was going to happen next. The girls were already tired of laughing and they sat crumbling cakes between their fingers to find out—as they said—what was inside them. When the table in front of them was full of crumbs, and even their party dresses were full of crumbs, they began whispering and giggling together about Masha's dress and her mother who plucked chickens in the marketplace.

Friedman grew tired and his eyes began to water. He looked at Hadassah and Borochov sitting with downcast eyes and trying to pretend that it all had nothing to do with them, and suddenly he shouted, "Oy, Hadassah, my Hadassah! When I look at you like this, in your white bridal gown, with your bright black eyes, oy, my Hadassah! You're not yourself now, you're your mother! Your mother who died so long ago. Why did she die, why didn't she live to see you marry such a fine, respectable husband? Hadassah is marrying the teacher Borochov, head of the cultural committee of the colony!"

The old man cupped his hands around his mouth, lifted his face to the sky, and trumpeted, "Esther, my Esther, you hear me? Our Hadassah is marrying the teacher Borochov, head of the cultural committee! If only you could hear the Hebrew he speaks! A person can't understand a single word!"

Friedman bowed his head, spread out his hands, and threw himself onto the table. No one knew if he had fallen asleep or if he was soundlessly weeping, for his shoulders seemed to be shaking.

The musicians packed up their instruments and the teacher Borochov ran after them and pushed sweets and cakes into their pockets. The garden was almost empty. Only Friedman and the cart drivers sat sprawled over the tables. A few guests, more courageous than their fellows, went up to the bride and groom to wish them *mazeltov*.

Weiss stood up with his family and approached the teacher Borochov and his wife. Weiss kissed Borochov on his pink cheek and urged him to bring his wife to visit them in their house on Train Street. Bracha shook the bride and groom by the hand and tears poured down her face. She went up to Chasida too, who was also crying, and tried to see what kind of a woman she was. The girls smiled sweetly at the bride and groom and pressed their father to hurry up and take them home.

Hadassah said to Borochov, "He spoilt our celebration. At the beginning everybody was so happy."

The teacher Borochov stroked her tender hand and said, "Never mind, Hadassah, it's late already anyway."

"Your cousins sat and laughed shamelessly all the time," said Hadassah. "I saw them, but I pretended not to see."

"Look," said Borochov, "Masha is helping your Aunt Chasida to clear the tables."

"I told you she was a good girl," said Hadassah.

AT TWO O'CLOCK in the morning they heard the beadle calling the people in the Yemenite quarter to *selichot*, the penitential prayers in the days preceding the Day of Atonement. The beadle of the Yemenite synagogue had a powerful voice, clear as the nights of *Elul*.

"Come and pra-a-y!" he called, drawing out the last syllable with all the air in his lungs, and his voice reverberated like distant thunder and filled the night air.

Hadassah stood next to the window. The cool air caressed her face and the jasmine bushes rustled in the breeze.

"They're calling the people to prayer in the Yemenite quarter," said Hadassah.

"Yes," said her husband. "Soon the holidays will be here, and then the winter."

"It's growing cool already, Yedidya. It's the end of summer," said Hadassah.

"The end of summer," smiled the teacher Borochov sadly, "the season of love is over."

The cool night breeze filled the room with the intoxicating scent of the jasmine and the sound of the ram's horn blowing in the Yemenite quarter. The season of love was over.

· 8 ·

BEFORE THE HOLIDAYS THE SUMMER DRAWS TO AN END. THE fruit swells on the trees, but it is still green.

At first Haim Weiss spent a lot of time walking around his

47

new orange grove, with Baruch explaining the way the work was going. Weiss trusted Nechama's Baruch. In the meantime there was no income from the grove, and Weiss had to pay Baruch and the Arabs out of his pocket, but he was sure that in the spring he would make a fortune.

Nechama's Baruch was not like the other overseers. Although he worked as hard as any of the Arabs, Weiss had to do the accounts himself, because he didn't trust Baruch to do them. It wasn't that he suspected him of dishonesty, but just that arithmetic held fewer mysteries for him.

Weiss would walk about the orange grove, feeling the green balls, breathing in the coolness of the dark trees with their heavy foliage, looking contentedly at the Arabs busy hoeing and irrigating. For the time being there wasn't much work, until the picking season came, and with it the sorting, packing, and transporting.

But as the summer came to a close, Weiss began waiting more and more tensely for the picking period that was approaching and became ready to put himself to the test of a real citrus farmer. After lengthy negotiations which he conducted himself, old Levin agreed to let him draw water from his well. He had already grown used to dressing like the other farmers, but he refused to ride on a donkey and despised the farmers jolting up and down on the backs of the ugly beasts.

Toward the end of summer the sky clouded over because the Nile was rising. They weren't rain clouds, the first rain would fall only after the High Holidays. The daylight darkened and people raised their eyes to the sky to see the Nile clouds floating above them.

In the afternoon the neighbor women sat on the bench outside Nechama's house. They too looked up at the sky to see the Nile clouds and the dying of the summer. Baruch returned from the orange grove and heard his mother talking to her neighbors.

Nechama said, "My Baruch is picky. He's like his father, God rest his soul. Any old girl won't do for him."

The neighbor women looked at her with forgiving smiles and nodded their heads in agreement.

Baruch was already thirty-five or forty years old and he still wasn't married. At first he had worked at digging pits in the citrus grove. He would go to work at dawn and come home in the early evening. Now Mr. Weiss had made him his overseer. Nechama said, "My Baruch isn't a simple laborer. He's an overseer. One day he'll have citrus groves of his own, and other people will be his overseers."

Baruch bathed, changed his clothes, and stood at the window to watch the passersby in the street and listen to his mother talking to her neighbors.

When the neighbor women went home to their suppers, Baruch sat on the bench in the darkness to escape his mother's nagging and waited for his room to cool down so that he could go to bed.

Baruch was hefty, fair-haired, and freckled. His little eyes had no lashes and his hands were huge and bony. When the children teased him with their questions, he would pick up a heavy stone from the side of the road, look at them with hate, and then throw the stone down angrily at his feet.

When his mother began one of her long and tedious sermons, he would stand opposite her with downcast eyes, patient and dumb.

Nechama said to him, "What are you waiting for, Baruch? Pick yourself a girl and marry her. The neighbors ask me every day why you don't get married and they think all kinds of things. Look, Masha's still free. She's a modern girl and she's got a steady job at the sweet factory. Go and ask her to walk out with you. You'll both work and between the two of you, you'll manage nicely."

But Baruch did not reply. His mother looked at him and

she knew that he had not taken her words to heart. She went angrily into her room and slammed the door behind her. And Baruch went to his room and to bed.

Baruch could not fall asleep. It was still hot in the room and the cats were howling under his window. He got up and stood in front of the window. The night sky was very light and the Nile clouds had disappeared. He saw the cats in heat underneath his window, arching their backs, wailing in longing, despair, and rage.

Then some girls from the training farm went past in a cart. He didn't see them; he only heard the horses' hooves and the creaking of the shafts, the merry laughter and soft singing of the girls lying on the bottom of the cart:

> And the girls who go down to the vineyards,
> And the girls who go down to the grape vines,
> Their eyes are dark as night,
> Their eyes are dark as night,
> Oh the night, oh the night . . .
> *Ya-layil, ya-layil . . .*

Baruch closed the window, leaped into bed, and covered his eyes with both huge hands.

Years before, Baruch had decided to build himself a house in the yard. Nechama said to the neighbors sitting on the bench, "My Baruch has decided not to get married until he's built himself a house."

When he came home from Mirkin's citrus grove, he would retire to the yard and work on the house. All the neighbors thought that after he had finished building the house he would bring a girl to live in it. Baruch would stand in the yard digging holes for the foundations, leveling the ground, sawing planks, and pouring cement. He did most of the work himself, hiring workers from Birzha only when it was absolutely necessary.

On his way home from work he would linger next to the Sports League gym and peep through the high windows to see the girls doing their exercises. Once they caught him at it and he ran away in disgrace. Ever since then he would take roundabout routes and keep out of sight. And thus the beaten, persecuted, hangdog expression crept into his eyes.

Nechama said to her neighbors on the bench, "My Baruch is like his father, he's got golden hands. When the building is finished he'll bring the girl."

But the building was already finished and Baruch brought no girl. He bought saplings and planted fruit trees in the yard, separating his mother's house from his new, empty one.

Nechama said to her neighbors, "When Baruch's fruit trees grow he'll bring the girl." But the neighbors already knew that the trees would grow tall and blossom and give fruit and shed fruit and Nechama's Baruch would bring no girl.

The neighbor women sat on Nechama's bench and asked her, "How's Baruch?"

And Nechama replied, "My Baruch would never take any old girl off the street. The girl he picks will be treated like a princess. My Baruch is like his father, God rest his soul, picky."

Baruch furnished his house. The vines climbed up the porch and reached the roof. The shutters were painted bright green. The whole house was new and shining, but there was no girl in it.

Baruch now saw the sad eyes of his mother, who scarcely spoke to him, and he understood that she was angry with him. He hardly ever went into the new house, and in his mother's presence he could not escape her eyes. He bought himself a young donkey.

When night fell he left the house. He would go to the big haystack and stand at a little distance. He would see the boys and girls lying together in the hay and his heart would contract. One of the boys played the harmonica, and others responded in chorus: "Oh the night, oh the night—*Ya-layil, ya-layil* . . . " Baruch heard their laughter and sighs and coughs and he swallowed every murmur thirstily. Evening after evening he went back. He knew all the tunes of the harmonica almost by heart, the notes of the refrain *"Ya-layil,"* and even the voices of the dogs from the Arab villages borne on the evening winds.

Nechama said to her neighbors, "My Baruch goes out every evening to enjoy himself with the girls on the haystack. He comes back late at night. I think he'll have a surprise for me after the holidays."

One evening Baruch waited next to Masha's house. Every evening at seven she would go out for a walk around the village. He hid behind the old packing shed, and when she came out he followed her silently down the acacia avenue. When they reached the road he quickened his pace, approached her, and whispered into her ear:

"Masha."

Masha turned her head and looked at him as if he had fallen off the moon.

"What do you want here, Baruch?" she asked.

"I want to go for a walk with you," replied Baruch, blinking his eyes in excitement. He remembered his mother waiting for him at home.

Masha inspected him from top to toe with her angry eyes, as if she thought he had taken leave of his senses. Baruch took the little bottle of scent he had bought in the village out of his pocket and offered it to Masha. She took the scent from his hand, looked at him, and pretended that she didn't know what was inside the bottle.

"What's this you've brought me?" she asked.

"It's perfume," said Baruch. "I bought it specially for you. In the village they said you liked to use it."

Masha said in a hostile voice, "What do you want of me?"

Baruch pleaded, "Let's go for a walk together, Masha! Please!"

"Where do you want to go for a walk?"

"To the haystack. They all lie on the hay there and they sing and there's a smell of damp hay, and the dogs barking . . ."

Masha laughed. "You're not normal. I won't go with you to the haystack. Everybody knows me there and I'd be ashamed to go there with you."

Baruch didn't understand. Or he pretended not to understand. But he didn't say anything. He looked at Masha and he didn't know if she was pretty or ugly. He only knew that she had a flat chest and she tried to hide it. She said to him, "So where do you want to go?"

"To the citrus groves," Baruch compromised.

They walked in the direction of the citrus groves and turned into a path between the trees, and Baruch heard the jackals wailing. It seemed to him that they too were singing "*Ya-layil, ya-layil*, wail, wail . . ." and that the wind was playing the harmonica between the branches of the trees. But all he could think about was the haystack and the bottle of perfume he had given Masha for nothing.

They went deep into the groves; one grove came to an end and a second began, and between each grove and the next there was a row of cypresses or an acacia hedge. Masha nearly tore her dress on a hedge. She was already short of breath and she was tired of walking. But Baruch thought they should go farther. Until they reached the end of all the orange groves in the world, thought Masha.

When Masha had had enough, she asked him, "Where do you think you're taking me? I'm tired."

Baruch couldn't decide. He wanted to go on walking, and his legs were as strong as ever. Masha lost her temper and started running away from him in the direction of the road. He ran after her. He started wailing like the cats at night under his window. She screamed at him, "Madman! Freak!" She was tired and she didn't have the strength to escape. Baruch caught up with her and seized her by the arm.

"Masha," he said.

Masha took the bottle of perfume from her bag and threw it furiously onto the road. The tiny bottle shattered and broke. Baruch was astounded. She extricated herself from the vise of his arms and ran away. Baruch felt as if he had been turned to stone. He touched the little puddle sinking into the road with his finger, raised his finger to his nose, and breathed with all the power of his lungs. Then he lay down on the road, stuck his nose into the scent, and smelled it for a long time.

Masha disappeared into the darkness. The sound of her running died away.

Nechama said to her neighbors on the bench, "My Baruch is going around with Masha. Yesterday he gave her a bottle of perfume for a present."

The neighbor women winked at one another and smiled back at her hypocritically.

Baruch went to work in the orange grove that morning, and he didn't speak a word to anyone all day. In the evening he was supposed to go to Weiss's house to report on the preparations for the approaching picking season, but he decided not to go. He came home from work. He walked around the yard among the fruit trees. The guava trees were loaded with fruit and their intoxicating scent filled the yard, for it was already autumn. He stood for a long time next to the stable he had built, stroking his donkey. Then he walked around the fruit trees again, smelling the guavas. The yard was beginning to look neglected. There were no neat basins anymore and the couch grass had already spread its net between the trees. But Baruch didn't care. His mother came into the yard and asked him with a smile, "Aren't you going to take a shower before you go out this evening?"

Baruch said, "Yes." He went into his room and he didn't know what to do. In the end he went to take a shower. He stayed in the shower and he didn't want to come out. His mother was alarmed and she began calling him from the other side of the door. Baruch answered her in a weak voice. She begged him to come out, but he refused. She threatened to break the door down with an axe. She stood outside the door banging on it with her fists and crying. She called the neighbors and they began to unscrew the hinges. Then Baruch gave in and came out.

"What's the matter with you?" asked his frightened mother. "You're so pale. Are you ill?"

"Yes, Mother, I'm ill," said Baruch.

He lay on his bed. His mother said that perhaps he was suffering from sunstroke. But he replied that it was nothing and there was no need to call the doctor.

All night long he couldn't sleep. Only toward morning did the room grow cool and he closed his eyes. He slept for about an hour and woke up refreshed, washed himself, and hurried to the orange grove. On the way he rode his donkey to Mr. Weiss's house. He told him that the day before he had been unwell, and then he rode to the grove and worked all day as usual. His mother talked about the new house and about his donkey, and the neighbor women sat next to her on the bench and smiled hypocritical smiles.

· 9 ·

IN THE MIDDLE OF THE PICKING SEASON LANGFUSS THE BROKER came to visit the Weiss family.

Weiss was in high spirits. He had spent the afternoon

taking the girls for a tour of the orange grove and explaining the work to them. They had not shown any special interest and he had taken this as a sign that they were trying to annoy him. He stroked the fruit with his fingers as if he were stroking a beloved woman. In the packing shed the sorters sat sorting the fruit. The wrappers from the women's training farm wrapped the fruit so rapidly that their fingers blurred as they rolled it up in the tissue paper which smelled of preservatives. The packers put the wrapped fruit in the crates, nailed down the lids, and stamped them with big, sharp-smelling stamps whose letters shone like gold. Others rapidly shouldered the crates and arranged them in rows. Weiss felt that he was in his prime again. He strode back and forth with an air of importance, his hands folded behind his back, asking questions, giving instructions, and examining every nook and cranny. Baruch basked in his employer's satisfaction and exerted himself to explain everything in his inarticulate way.

Langfuss had chosen a good time for his visit. Since Weiss had taken up residence in his new house, he had paid them only rare, brief visits, always to discuss matters of business. He wanted to persuade Weiss to add a few small groves to his property.

It was already winter. The first rain had come down heavily for a few days and stopped. The days grew fine again. But the nights were unpleasantly chilly and damp. Weiss offered Langfuss something strong to drink, but the broker preferred a glass of tea. Bracha went out to make the tea. Langfuss took out a packet of cigarettes, offered it to Weiss, and lit the two cigarettes with his shining silver lighter.

There was a moment of silence during which Langfuss sat scratching his square black mustache with his fingernail. Bracha came in with tea and cake. She avoided meeting the broker's eyes, which frightened her, put the things down on the table, asked him coldly to help himself, and retired immediately to the little kitchen, where she sat and warmed her hands over the paraffin ring and boiling kettle.

Batsheva sat in the big room reading a novel, as if there were nobody there but herself. Langfuss thought that she had something against him and was about to get up and leave, but Weiss made him sit down again, hung his hat on the hat stand, and said to Batsheva, "Is your book so interesting that you can't put it down?"

Batsheva smiled at them sweetly, closed the book calmly after first placing a bookmark between the pages, and looked at them with an expectant expression. Since nobody said anything, she broke the silence herself. "And how are you, Mr. Langfuss? Who is selling something? Who is buying something?"

Langfuss blushed and a pained expression crossed his face.

Weiss began to gabble, "What Batsheva needs is a job. It's not that she's bored, God forbid, or spends all day sitting at home with her sister reading novels—but she's a talented girl, she finished the gymnasium with honors. She's highly educated and she knows languages. Her talents should be put to use." Weiss turned to his daughter. "Your own father may praise you a little to your face, may he not, Batsheva?" he tried to placate her.

"If it raises the price of the goods—yes, he may," said Batsheva, and walked out of the room.

As usual when he was embarrassed, Langfuss removed his thick spectacles, took out his handkerchief, and began to polish the lenses. He wiped one lens, held it at arm's length to see if it was clean, did the same with the other, put his spectacles back on his nose, folded his handkerchief neatly, and replaced it in his jacket pocket with the tip peeping out.

Langfuss was dressed with wintry elegance. His shoes shone and his trousers were sharply creased. His mustache was neatly trimmed. He wore a thick gold ring with the letters

M and L on the ring finger of his left hand. He was a young man still, but he had the air of belonging to a different age. He took out a cigarette and lit it. This time he did not offer one to Weiss. Weiss asked him if he knew of a job for Batsheva.

"I have a friend who works in the Anglo-Palestine Bank," said Langfuss. "I believe they need girls who know foreign languages there."

Weiss took hold of his sleeve and looked at him imploringly. Langfuss promised that he would try. Riva came into the room and asked him how he was. She smiled at him in a friendly way.

"I don't understand what the matter is with Batsheva today," said Weiss, and looked at the other two as if they had the key to the secret.

Riva shrugged her shoulders. Langfuss got up to go. Outside it began to rain and the sky was full of lightning flashes.

"We'll lend you an umbrella, Mr. Langfuss," said Riva, and walked with him to the end of the passage. At the door she gave him the umbrella. He took his hat from the stand, put it on, and seemed about to say something. Riva opened the door and the sound of the rain drowned their voices.

"Mr. Langfuss, try to get a job for her. As quick as you can. Or she'll go out of her mind and drive the rest of us crazy too," she said, and closed the door behind him.

· 10 ·

ALL WINTER LONG BARUCH WORKED AS THE OVERSEER IN WEISS'S orange grove, and Weiss was very satisfied with him. He said little, worked in the grove like one of the Arabs, and came to Weiss once a week in the evening to report. After the excitement of the picking was over, Weiss did not go often to his grove. The income from the fruit was excellent and he began to dream of new groves. Their household expenses were few. Bracha did all the housework, and he did not take a maid to help her, not even to prepare for the Sabbath on Fridays. The girls too did nothing in the house. Batsheva began to work in the bank and came home in the afternoon, and Riva worked at the sewing shop in the colony. Langfuss had arranged it all for them.

Weiss spent most of his days doing nothing. He would escape from the house in order not to hear Bracha's bitter sighs as she bent over to wash the floor or beat the bedclothes, wander about the colony, and go to the "labor exchange" looking for companions for an idle chat.

Bracha rose in the morning before everyone else and set to work immediately. She made a lot of noise and her family grumbled about her in secret, under their breath, so that she would not know she was disturbing them and derive any pleasure from the knowledge. Bracha stopped her usual complaining, and her faded blue eyes sunk in their sea of wrinkles sent them venomous looks.

When they sat at home in the evenings, she would make them all get up so she could polish the legs of the chairs they were sitting on. Whenever anyone came into their house, she followed behind him to wipe away his footprints with a damp cloth. Her silence was worse than her complaints. The father and the two daughters stood facing her like a wall of hatred.

After the teacher Borochov married Hadassah, he too lost his charms in Bracha's eyes, and he too was greeted with the same empty looks and obsessive footprint cleaning when he came one day to pay them a courtesy call.

At night Bracha would beg her dead father and mother to take pity on her and save her from the murderers. She would weep softly and the other members of the household would stiffen in their beds with rage.

The trees Baruch planted in the yard grew. Around the fence he had planted a row of rhododendrons, pink and white alternately, and they bloomed in the spring and brightened the approach to the house. Baruch came frequently to water the trees, weed, hoe, and fertilize. The rain had stopped falling, and the dry, hot winds heralding the summer compacted the red soil and cut deep fissures in it. The citrus groves were in blossom all around and they flooded the air with their sweet, intoxicating scent attractive with swarms of bees.

Once again Nechama's neighbors sat outside on her bench and asked her, "And how is Baruch?"

Baruch spent his afternoons with his donkey, grooming it and stroking it for hours on end. His mother was at her wits' end.

"Mr. Weiss has bought more groves," she said to them. "And my Baruch is the overseer of them all. Weiss has raised his salary."

"And how's Masha?" they asked.

"Masha? Is that the girl for my Baruch? A loose woman! They went out together for a while, until Baruch saw that she wasn't the girl for him."

The neighbors smiled understandingly. They had decided among themselves that Baruch was keeping his donkey in the new house he had built for his bride. They pressed Nechama to show them the new house, hoping that they would find the donkey there, or at least a few turds in a corner. But Nechama refused. Only one woman will enter that house, she said, one woman and one woman only. When? the neighbors would ask. And Nechama would shake her head and say with a bitter smile, "After the holidays, God willing."

BARUCH WORKED IN Weiss's yard in the afternoon, but the sun still blazed down on him slantwise from the sky. He stood with the upper half of his body naked, hitting the dry red soil strongly and rhythmically with his hoe. His chest was covered with blond hairs, his back muscular and freckled. The sweat trickled over the hairs on his chest and dripped from his armpits.

Riva came out of the house, stared at him in amazement, and sat down on the balustrade of the veranda, where she continued looking fixedly at him. Baruch felt her eyes on him and shivers ran down his spine. He put the hoe down and pulled up his trousers, enough to cover his navel at least. He resumed his hoeing, his navel was exposed again, and he felt a great and desperate shame.

He realized that Riva was only pretending to look at the scenery while she peeped at his broad shoulders out of the corner of her eye. Gradually he was filled with pride at his muscular shoulders and solid chest, and he slowed down the rhythm of his hoeing, bending and straightening up gracefully, trying to catch Riva's eyes with his little, lashless eyes. He put the hoe down and leaned it against the fence. He knelt down next to the basin he had dug and began to pull out the couch grass.

He felt as if Riva's eyes were boring little holes in his throat. Now a great heat replaced the shivers and spread through his body, and his hands began to sweat and tremble, and he realized that he couldn't get up and stand on his feet without disgracing himself. His heart pounded madly, and he was afraid that he might be going out of his mind.

The sun receded, and when dusk fell he was still kneeling next to the basin in the ground. It occurred to him to surround the whole yard with a deep trench to get rid of the couch grass, rake up all the stones from the garden, and fertilize the trees again. Plans. But in the meantime he was still crouching next to the hole in the ground, one hand groping desperately among the clods of earth in search of another blade of grass, the other stroking his hairy chest and armpit.

It was almost dark, but Riva was still sitting on the veranda and looking at him, and he went on fumbling in the basin and feeling that the only way he could stand up would be to jump to his feet and run a very long way to cool his boiling blood.

He pulled himself together, stood up, put on his shirt with his back to Riva, and ran off like a madman without saying goodbye. He ran past the groves where he worked and reached old Levin's groves, panting and out of breath. This was the roundabout way he came every day, ever since he had been caught red-handed looking through the windows of the gym. But instead of turning right onto the road leading to the colony, he went on running toward the fields.

It was still twilight. On the horizon red and green flames burned above the distant mountains. A little Arab girl stood in the middle of the field gathering her herd of black and brown goats together to take them home to her village. She spoke to them, scolded them, and hit them with a stick to goad them. There was no one in sight. The only sound was the melancholy chugging of the well engine in the distance.

Baruch set upon her in the field and did a terrible thing to her.

When he came to his senses he found himself lying in the field among the thorns and the dung, the panic-stricken goats running to and fro around him, bleating deafeningly. His eyes saw only death and blood and rags and black stains.

He felt neither sorrow nor dread, only a great, enclosed emptiness and a broken heart. He wanted to stay there and close his eyes and fall asleep where he lay. And never to get up again.

In the end he got up, weak and shaken, and walked to the place where the road turned into the colony. There he remembered that he had left his donkey in Weiss's yard, and his blood froze in horror. He could not go back there. He did not know why, but his feet refused to budge. He was afraid to stay where he was too. If he went home on foot his mother would ask questions. He wavered for a long time, unable to make up his mind. His hands were shaking and he cursed his donkey roundly.

In the darkness he saw a cart coming toward him from the citrus groves. He jumped to one side and hid behind the bushes. It was a small, donkey-drawn cart, loaded with crates of fruit, and a bearded Yemenite with long earlocks was sitting on the driver's seat and humming softly in time to the jolting of the cart.

When the cart disappeared he came out of his hiding place. In his panic he had lost his sense of direction and he didn't know which way to go. He turned this way and that, leaned against a tree, and tried to think. It was very dark and the lights of the colony could not be seen from where he stood. The citrus groves on the other side of the road huddled together like lumps of darkness, swarming with secrets and terrors. After a time he overcame his fears and started walking in the direction of Train Street. He met no one on his way. The lights were still on in Weiss's house, and he realized that it was not as late as he thought. There was no one in the yard or on the veranda, despite the heat. The donkey was still tethered to a pole in the fence, quietly nibbling the grass around him. Baruch untied him and put on his saddle without looking at him. He didn't give him even one touch of affection. He rode slowly along the short road to the colony. He passed the gym without being aware of it. In the street where he lived he saw his mother sitting with her neighbors on the bench. She hurried to meet him. When he came closer she asked anxiously, "What happened?"

"I stayed late at Weiss's house, I had to see him about work," lied Baruch without batting an eyelash.

The neighbors tried to suppress their laughter; Baruch

didn't know why they were laughing. Nechama's face twisted.

"Liar," his mother hissed through her teeth. "Mr. Weiss is sitting in our house this minute waiting for you. I'm ashamed to look him in the eye."

· 11 ·

"WHAT DAY IS IT TODAY, BARUCH?" ASKED WEISS AS SOON AS Baruch walked into the room.

"What day is it today, Mr. Weiss?" Baruch didn't understand the question. "I don't know what kind of a day it is today."

Weiss sat in the big room on one of the black chairs standing around the table. Baruch's father's big clock was ticking. Weiss looked at him with a stern but smiling face. Baruch didn't understand that this old man felt affection for him.

"Today is Thursday, Baruch."

"Right, Mr. Weiss, I forgot that today is Thursday."

"What's the matter, Baruch? Don't you feel well?"

"No, Mr. Weiss."

"You're pale and shaking as if you've got malaria."

"Maybe I've got malaria, I don't know anything."

"Sunstroke!" said Weiss. "Sunstroke. You don't take care in the sun, Baruch."

Baruch said nothing and waited for Weiss to go. He didn't even wonder why Weiss had taken the trouble to come to his house. Then he remembered that Thursday was the day when he was to stay late to report on the work in the grove.

"Go to bed for a few days, Baruch, until you feel better," said Weiss. "In any case there's not much work in the grove now." He smiled at Baruch and made ready to leave. Near the door he paused, as if there were something else he wanted to say. He looked anxiously around and discovered that Baruch was already lying on the couch with his eyes shut.

"Excuse me, Mr. Weiss, for behaving like this in front of you," he mumbled, "but my head's spinning and I feel bad."

Weiss came back and stood at the head of the couch. Baruch's eyes were still closed, and his smooth lids quivered. Baruch felt Mr. Weiss breathing at his head. He tried to smile, but he couldn't manage it.

Weiss couldn't find the words to comfort his overseer. Baruch's mother came and stood in the passage door, waiting for Weiss to leave. In the end Weiss took his courage in his hands and stroked the frizzy flaxen head. "Be well, Baruch," he said. "I can't do anything without you. I'm sure you'll feel better soon."

As soon as Weiss left, Nechama came into the room. Baruch tried to open his eyes. His mother said, "What happened, Baruch? I want to know everything."

"Nothing happened."

"I know there's something wrong," she insisted.

"Go to bed," he said.

"All the neighbors know that you're a liar now."

"Let all the neighbors go to hell," said Baruch, and turned onto his side.

"Stop cursing, you hear!"

"Leave me alone. I want to die."

"Baruch," said his mother, "I took the donkey in and fed it."

"Let him go to hell too."

"Stop cursing, I told you."

"You can go to hell too, with all the rest of them."

WHEN WEISS WENT out of Nechama's house, his anger had completely left him. The sight of Baruch's suffering had dissolved a wall of obstinacy in him. His resolution to use force against the Jewish workers who had announced their intention of picketing his citrus grove the next day as a protest against his employment of cheap Arab labor drained away in the hot summer evening. Weiss walked slowly, sunk in thought. When he reached Friedman's house he quickened his pace and hurried past, for fear of succumbing to the temptation of going in and asking the head of the cultural committee for help. His self-confidence returned and the obvious solution came to him in a flash: He would behave like all the other farmers, call in the police, and put an end to the affair without giving himself any trouble. Suddenly the whole world seemed full of goodness to him, all its inhabitants kind and contented, as if he had had too much to drink.

He couldn't understand it. Tonight of all nights, with the streets full of suffocating heat, not a leaf stirring, everything covered in dust and sweat. Tomorrow morning the police would come to beat up the pickets, a fight would break out, abuse would be shouted, while Baruch, good kind Baruch, lay ill, his smooth eyelids trembling with pain. A pure, simple soul, reflected Weiss painfully, perhaps the last of a race of giants. One day everyone would look like the teacher Borochov, Talmudic scholars who had abandoned the articles of their faith but had remained as idle as ever.

Friedman the drunk suddenly came stumbling toward him, a sour smell of wine enveloping him like a fog. Friedman was walking alone and unsupported. Weiss tried to slip away, but the drunk saw him and tottered toward him.

"There'll be fun and games here tomorrow morning!" shouted Friedman.

Weiss was not sure that Friedman knew what he was saying. He ignored him and continued on his way.

"In-law!" cried Friedman after him. "In-law! Don't you say hello anymore?"

Weiss continued calmly on his way.

He had no friends among the farmers of the colony, he thought. If he had any, he would have gone to ask their advice. They kept him at arm's length, and he didn't know why. Everything receded and grew blurred. His feet carried him to Train Street. That damned Langfuss was probably there now, courting Batsheva. Ever since he had obtained that job for her at the bank he kept coming to visit them. He wasn't put off by her sarcasm. He sat there smiling at her, as if her barbs were not directed at him.

But Langfuss was not there. Bracha was in bed again, with all the winter blankets piled on top of her. *Mazeltov!* That was all he needed now. Riva and Batsheva were sitting on the veranda overlooking the yard, recovering from the heat.

"Has Langfuss been here?" asked Weiss.

"No, thank God," said Batsheva.

"She's dying again," said Riva.

"She's found the right time for it," grumbled Weiss. "Tomorrow they're going to picket my orange grove. The police are coming, there'll be fighting, a whole commotion, and my Baruch is sick. Even Langfuss the omnipotent can't help me now."

"Langfuss?" laughed Batsheva. "What can poor Langfuss do?"

Bracha called out from her room. Riva went inside, and when she came out again she said, "She's praying."

Weiss clenched his fists in irritation. The next day Baruch did not come to work. Weiss called the police and watched them beat up the pickets from a safe distance. He did not interfere, encourage the police, or thank them. When it was all over the Arabs went into the grove and continued their work as usual. Weiss remained in the orange grove, hanging about as long as possible so as not to have to go home to the sick Bracha.

At midday Riva came running to the grove and told him that they would have to fetch a doctor. He sent her to summon the doctor and went home, where he found Bracha burning with fever. There was no one at home and Weiss made her some tea. Riva returned from the colony, frightened and perspiring. The doctor would be there soon, she said, and she herself would stay home to look after her mother.

The doctor came and examined Bracha but he could not get a word out of her. Weiss told him about her behavior over the past few years. The doctor spent a long time examining her; then he prescribed some medicine.

The next day Bracha felt better. She regained consciousness and with it the usual talk about her impending death and the daughters she would not live to see married. During the week that followed, her recovery proceeded apace, but she kept to her bed and continued to suffer from the cold.

Baruch came back to work after a few days, and Weiss hardly recognized him. He was worn out, weak, and feeble, his eyes were swollen as if he had been crying, and his hands shook.

ONE SATURDAY MORNING at the end of *Elul* it began to rain. Rain in the middle of summer! Everyone went outside to see the wonder. But in the big synagogue Shor the Monk suddenly rose in his seat, went up to the pulpit, and delivered an impassioned sermon. Shor the Monk was a tall, red-haired man. His hair grew wild and his red beard was long and frizzy. He would often go up to the pulpit and make speeches, taking no notice of the protests and scornful cries of the congregation. They were usually obliged to remove him by force as he refused to climb down of his own accord before concluding his long addresses. He would denounce the foreign rulers, the obsequious and cowardly leaders of the Jewish *Yishuv*, the farmers and the workers and the Arabs. He spoke with his eyes shut.

The Monk went up to the pulpit and pointed to the windows dripping with rain. "Has anybody ever heard of such a thing? Rain in the middle of summer, rain in the month of *Elul*?" he asked the congregation, waving his finger threateningly in the air. "Rain in the middle of the Days of Penitence, an omen for the Day of Atonement! The Day of Atonement is at hand and nobody pays any heed. It is the finger of God!"

Members of the congregation abused him and told him to stop wasting their time and interfering with their prayers. But the Monk was oblivious, as if there were a fire burning in his bones. "Thousands of corrupt, immoral people are streaming into the country," he said, "riff-raff, desecrators of the Sabbath, beggars, roaming the colonies and inciting people. Rabble-rousers, trespassers, troublemakers, saboteurs . . ."

The congregation shouted that they hadn't come to the synagogue to hear political speeches, the synagogue on the Sabbath was no place for politics. But the Monk clung to the pulpit railing with both hands and said that he would not be budged from where he stood. "Look at the rain!" he cried. "Rain in *Elul*. Who has ever seen the like? It's these workers, sinners causing others to sin, ruining the atmosphere in the country . . ."

The elderly rabbi now approached him and insisted in no uncertain terms that he climb down. Shor the Monk gave in, shrugged his shoulders, and said, "You're all my witnesses that I spoke up and did not hold my peace. May the Lord have mercy on us on this coming Day of Atonement."

Toward noon the sky cleared and the rest of the day was an ordinary summer's day.

BRACHA WEISS'S CONDITION worsened again. In the citrus groves opposite the house, the picking season was in full swing. The carts rumbled back and forth over the roads, loaded with crates of fruit, and girls from the training farm sat in them and sang. The days were fresh and everything was green as far as the eye could see. The season was a good one, the fruit was plentiful, and the profits high.

One morning they found Bracha Weiss lying under the blankets they had piled on top of her, her face yellow and her eyes staring. Riva screamed and Weiss closed the dead woman's eyes.

· 12 ·

ONLY A FEW PEOPLE CAME TO CALL ON THEM DURING THE DAYS of mourning. Langfuss came the day after the funeral and sat with them for an hour or so. Old Levin came on his donkey. He stood in front of Weiss for a few minutes, mumbled something indistinctly, and departed as abruptly as he had arrived. Baruch came almost every day, and Weiss did not know why.

From the day Weiss had seen him at his mother's house, Baruch had begun to shrink. His eyes were red and puffy from lack of sleep, and fear gnawed at his body and soul. Every shadow flitting past his bedroom window made his blood freeze. He lay wakeful in his bed counting the passing hours. Next to his bed he kept a big axe. Everything that happened seemed to him a portent of the retribution to come. He made his way to Weiss's orange grove like a man pursued by furies, and when he arrived he was weak and breathless.

During the days of mourning he presented himself at Weiss's house almost every day and stood there without a word. Weiss asked him how he was and Baruch replied, "Thank you very much, Mr. Weiss."

"And how is your mother?"

"Thank you very much, Mr. Weiss. She's sorry she can't come herself. It's too far for her old legs. But she came to the funeral."

Alarmed by this reference to death in his words, Baruch fell silent.

Weiss asked about the picking, the transport, and the wages. Baruch stammered brief replies. Weiss did not ask much. He looked at his daughters sitting on the floor in their stockings and reading their novels, but it was the boy who concerned him. He was weakening, shrinking, fading away before his eyes, as if he had suddenly turned into an old man. Weiss could not understand what the matter with Baruch was, and it upset him.

On the Sabbath which fell during the days of mourning Langfuss came again. It occurred to Weiss that the circle of his friends and acquaintances was smaller than he had imagined. Did he have to wait for Bracha's death to have this brought home to him? Through no fault of their own, he and his daughters were beyond the pale of the life of the colony, as isolated as the house they lived in.

He could no longer endure the sight of the moldy, peeling walls of the house in Train Street, the loneliness at night among the citrus groves. Bracha was dead. But her bitterness lingered on, hanging like cobwebs from the doors and windows and in the corners of the rooms. Now that she was dead he sat and pondered, trying to get to the bottom of her capricious moods and her melancholy. Her absence filled him with trivial, pointless memories, like the memory of little movements to which he had become accustomed. He tried to examine the nature of the limb that had been cut off from him, and he wondered if the amputation would save the rest of the body.

The girls sat with him in the big room and read their novels. A good thing there were books in the world, reflected Weiss. The girls had brought a big parcel of books with them from abroad, which they read over and over again. Weiss had never read a novel in his life. He knew that novels were written for women. He had never even felt any desire to pick one up and find out what it was all about. He thought that it might be better to separate the girls. When they were together some kind of devil seemed to get into them, especially Batsheva. There was something of her dead mother in her, in her blue-gray eyes, in the spite she spread around her. Only she did it with more charm.

On Saturday night Hadassah and Borochov came to visit them. Hadassah's heavy tread and a slight swelling in her face and body made Weiss suspicious. Borochov blushed in embarrassment at their scrutiny. The two girls put down their books and stared inquisitively.

The teacher Borochov said, "We're still suffering from the shock of the tragedy."

"I remember how kind she always was to us," said Hadassah.

Weiss could no longer control himself. "There'll be a new addition to your family soon," he said, and winked at Borochov.

The teacher blushed and Hadassah smiled proudly.

"How's the picking going?" asked Borochov.

"Thank God," said Weiss. "It's not over yet, but for the time being I can't complain. But we haven't had any rain this year and that Levin takes a lot of money for the water in his well."

"Never mind," said Borochov, "the winter isn't over yet."

Riva put on the light in the room. Up to then they had been sitting in the dark.

"Is the Sabbath over already?" asked Weiss.

The girls stared at him in astonishment. "I don't understand why it should bother you," said Batsheva.

"When is it due?" Weiss asked the teacher Borochov.

"What?" asked Borochov.

"Hadassah, when is she expecting the happy event?"

"There's still plenty of time," smiled Hadassah.

"I wish you good health," said Weiss.

"Perhaps you'll have twins?" said Batsheva.

"No, no," said Hadassah.

The teacher said, "Hadassah, we must be on our way."

"What's your hurry?" asked Weiss. "You said there's still plenty of time."

Everyone laughed. "Yedidya has homework to correct," said Hadassah.

Weiss saw them to the door. When he came back to the room, the girls were reading their novels again.

"Friedman the drunk's daughter is going to have a baby and my daughters sit reading novels," he sighed.

"Not everyone is lucky enough to have a father like hers," said Batsheva.

"It's a pity you weren't lucky enough to find a husband like hers," shouted Weiss.

"I still remember how you abused our sick mother when she said that he was the right man for me," said Riva.

"Me?" said Weiss indignantly. "Me? You were the one who was always laughing at him whenever he came here, you and your sister who sits there giving herself airs and reading her novel as if she can't hear us talking."

"You said he was a parasite and a loafer and a chatterbox," announced Batsheva.

"The pair of you were always laughing in his face and cutting him to pieces. I can still remember the way you behaved at his wedding."

"That doesn't change the fact that you opposed Mother, when it was almost the last favor she asked of me."

"Don't start trying to turn your mother into a saint. The three of us have nothing to hide from one another. You know as well as I do that she was sick in her head."

"You didn't show any consideration for her body either,"

said Batsheva. "Why didn't you take a maid to help her, at least on Fridays? You could see how she was collapsing right in front of our eyes, working like a slave from morning to night."

Weiss felt that he was going out of his mind. One man in a congregation of women—a foretaste of hell itself.

"Whatever I did was for your sakes, you fools, I thought only of you."

Riva, her eyes full of tears, said that she wished it was her who was dead instead of her mother.

AFTER THE MOURNING period was over, Langfuss dropped in again for a hasty visit. The moment he entered the house he sensed the tense atmosphere. Weiss's face was disfigured by a gray and white stubble. He asked him to sit down, and Langfuss saw that the old man really needed him for something. The girls were still sitting and reading. Weiss took hold of Langfuss's hand and led him into the little room.

"I need a new house," he said in a voice that Langfuss hardly recognized, like the voice of a drowning man crying for help. "Far away from here. I have money, I'll sell the small groves and buy a house in the middle of the colony. A fine big house with a garden. The main thing is to make the move soon. These girls are going to drive me out of my mind."

Weiss's confession embarrassed Langfuss. He explained that it couldn't be done from one day to the next, but he would do his best and let him know the results soon.

They returned to the big room. Outside the night was clear and cold. The shutters were closed and the house was stuffy and had a disagreeable smell. Langfuss was a squeamish man.

Weiss said to the girls, "I've decided to buy a big new house in the colony, a nice house with a garden."

"I don't know who would want to buy this house," said Langfuss. "Today people are afraid of living outside the colony."

"You'll find someone to buy it," protested Weiss. "You'll find someone. But we'll move even if you don't find a buyer. We can't go on living in this stable."

"Why not?" asked Batsheva.

"If you want to go on living here, you're welcome," said Weiss with suppressed anger.

"We've grown accustomed to this house," said Riva.

"You'll get used to another house too. It doesn't take long to grow accustomed to good things," said Langfuss, grabbing his hat and stick and beating a hasty retreat before the storm broke. Weiss accompanied him to the gate.

As soon as he left the room Batsheva said with a sour smile, "He's afraid of mother's memory in the rooms of this house and in the sooty little kitchen he squeezed her into."

Weiss came back into the room.

"Tomorrow I'll hire a maid," he said. "It's a long time since this place was cleaned."

"There's no need," said Riva, "I'll manage the work at the sewing shop and in the house too."

"Don't play the martyr, Riva," said Batsheva. "You can go on working at the sewing shop and he can hire a maid."

"In any case," said Weiss, "the maid will cost almost as much as Riva makes with her sewing. Maybe she's right."

"And needless to say," remarked Riva, "the work at the sewing shop isn't much pleasanter than housework, especially in summer. I don't work at the Anglo-Palestine Bank, Batsheva."

"But when we move to the new house . . ." said Batsheva.

"I see the idea is beginning to grow on you," smirked Weiss.

"But when we move to the new house," repeated Batsheva, "we'll need regular help. Big houses are a lot of work."

"But really," said Riva, "why should we move to a new house? Because mother never lived to see the day?"

"No," said Weiss, "because I, at least, want to see the pair of you married off, even if your mother never lived to see it. I've made up my mind to have that pleasure. I made a mistake when I bought this house. I didn't take into account that it's impossible to bring a young man here."

"It was you who wanted us to live outside the colony," Batsheva reminded him.

"I wanted to be close to the orange grove," said Weiss.

"That's not true," said Riva, "you bought the house first."

"You both know very well that I didn't want the whole colony to meet your mother. She wouldn't have done us any credit."

"Neither did this house do us any credit."

"Old maids," he suddenly screamed, "dried up old maids!"

"Not so old," said Batsheva with a scornful smile.

"And as for the rest," said Riva, "we can easily change that."

"Is that what you learned from your novels?"

"Yes," they replied in chorus.

"I thought that now we would have some peace and quiet in the house. A little more love and understanding between us."

"Why should it be more peaceful now?" asked Riva. "What's changed?"

"Nothing," said Weiss, "only that now we are three, and before we were four. I can remember how you used to incite me against her."

"And I suppose we refused to call the doctor when she lay in bed pleading for her life?" asked Batsheva.

"I couldn't bear to look into her eyes in the last months," said Riva. "She was full of wrinkles and her lips were thin and bitter. All your doing."

76

"When Batsheva is old," said Weiss, "she'll look like that too. She has her mother's eyes. And I'm beginning to discover similarities in her mind too. When your mother was young she was very like Batsheva."

"And I'm insane too, right? No, Father, you won't succeed in making me believe it, like you did Mother."

"Toward the end," said Riva, "she would call me to come and sit beside her. 'Tell me, Riva,' she would say to me, 'I'm not mad like your father says I am, am I? Your father has been trying to make me believe it all these years. But you all know the truth.' "

"What do you want?" exclaimed Weiss. "Now you'll drive me out of my mind like you did your poor mother. I know it was you two who did it to her."

"Don't answer him," said Batsheva to Riva.

"What do you want? Find yourselves husbands, get married, and leave me alone. I'll give you anything you ask for—houses, orange groves, money, everything I possess. Just leave me alone. I'll look after myself, I'll manage somehow. I'm not so old yet, I won't be helpless on my own. Who are you waiting for, the Messiah? If you're so clever and perfect, where are your suitors? I don't see them crowding at the door, I don't hear them calling and whistling for you. Nobody has come to ask me for your hands yet. My trouble is that I'm not Friedman the drunk. His daughter can get married, bear a child, be happy. Friedman the drunk will have grandchildren to climb onto his filthy lap and pull his wispy beard . . ."

He began to pace restlessly up and down the room. "I know what you're like—the barren shoots that grow from the roots and don't bear any fruit. You know what they call them here? Pigs! That's what you are, dry, bitter, barren old maids and God only knows what else!"

Batsheva got up with Riva behind her. They went into their room. None of them slept that night. They were afraid of the morning when they would have to meet each other face to face to behave as if nothing had happened and nothing had been said.

It was a long winter's night of the kind when nothing usually happens outside and the house is shuttered and barred against the world. Weiss wanted to weep in his bed and get rid of the pressure he had felt in his stomach and his temples ever since the day of Bracha's death, but he was unable to cry.

Batsheva and Riva did not open their mouths all night long, although they were both awake. They remembered the nights when Bracha imagined she was dying and they lay awake with their ears straining in the silence. But this time all they wanted was to shut their ears and not hear anything. They did not want to hear the sound of anyone breathing. All they wanted was to cuddle up in their heavy winter blankets and sink deeply into them. Neither of them understood the point of the quarrel or where it would lead, and the new house seemed to them like a fairytale told to a child to sweeten his sleep.

Riva was delighted at the prospect of stopping her work at the sewing shop. During the daytime hours, when Batsheva was away at work, she would be alone in the house with her father; she would be able to placate him, to retrieve his miserable love.

He forgot quickly, his heart was eager for any sign of warmth or understanding. More than that he did not ask of them. As for Batsheva, you could never do as you pleased in her presence, you weren't free to do anything under the scrutiny of those cold eyes. Riva now realized for the first time that however close she had been to people physically, to her parents and her sister, she did not know them at all. For the most part they matched only the rough outlines of a picture she had drawn of them in her mind. The main features were missing, but because of her physical closeness to them she had never felt the need for a clearer picture.

This realization terrified her. She remembered that her mother had always called them "murderers." What did she know about her father? And Batsheva? Nothing. Nothing except for the trivial, everyday things that revealed nothing. She was filled with terror at the thought of waking up one day and finding herself living in a house with total strangers who wished her ill and conspired against her. She peeped over her blankets at the woman lying in the bed on the other side of the room and forced herself to say in her heart, I know her well, I know her and love her. I knew her before she was born; before I myself was born her hand was already in mine. Batsheva, my good, gentle, beloved sister. Love is not acquired by habit, said Riva to herself, but by suffering. She tried to make herself suffer until she said "I love." She kissed her sister's blue eyes in her imagination, her slender, white, aristocratic hands. She saw Batsheva as her father's model of perfection, the need to love her as a debt she owed her dead mother.

Haim Weiss suddenly put the light on in his room and went into the kitchen to make himself a glass of tea with a dash of brandy. The light invading the house made Batsheva jump out of bed. Riva pretended to be asleep. Batsheva looked at her. Riva felt her sister's eyes on her and tried not to flutter her eyelids. Batsheva moved away from her bed and Riva heard her leaving the room.

In the kitchen Batsheva whispered to her father, "Don't you feel well, Father?"

"It's nothing, Batsheva."

"We were all mad. We are alone too much."

"I'm to blame for everything, Batsheva," sighed Weiss. "We have to get out of this house. It was madness on my part to insult you like that, to hurt your feelings."

They lowered their voices and Riva could not hear them. Her heart pounded, her bed began to burn, and she pushed the blankets down with her feet. Her face and body were bathed in sweat. The whispering in the kitchen next door made her shudder with revulsion and pain. It went on for a long time, very long, and in the end Riva imagined that it was all a nightmare, and she pinched herself and bit her tongue in the attempt to wake up.

At last she heard Batsheva's footsteps approaching the room. She covered herself immediately with her blankets and began breathing rhythmically. Batsheva got into bed and the light in her father's room went out.

Riva tried to fall asleep. She told herself what the new house would look like, but no picture appeared in her mind. All she could see in her imagination was a house composed of parts of the house on Train Street, and the whispering of her father and her sister went on buzzing between the peeling walls and setting her nerves on edge. The main thing was to remain lucid, thought Riva, to hang on and not to go mad. Nothing else mattered.

When she got up the next morning Batsheva was awake and moving about the house. Weiss had gone to the colony. Batsheva was full of smiles, as if nothing had happened the night before, and Riva exerted herself to emulate her, until Batsheva asked her in an indifferent tone of voice, "Are you feeling better, Riva? Have you calmed down since last night? You gave us a fright."

"I don't know what you're talking about," muttered Riva.

"Have you decided to stop work?"

"Yes. I'll go and tell them today."

"Father has gone to Langfuss about the new house."

"You're happy."

"Of course."

"Has he got enough money?"

"I couldn't care less."

Riva said nothing.

"I see," said Batsheva, "that you're not particularly excited."

"I'm afraid, afraid of change. I would prefer to stay here."

Batsheva combed her hair and Riva looked admiringly at her long, smooth, shining hair. Batsheva said goodbye to Riva and went to work.

Riva felt an urgent need to go out. Since they had run out of provisions, she decided to do some shopping in the big market. It was the first day of spring, fine and fragrant. The orange groves on either side of the dirt road were in blossom, and the rain puddles were drying up. She crossed the railway tracks and entered the main street of the colony. It was many days since she had seen a place so full of life and color and movement. From the railway line to the market, the street was lined with shops selling building materials, smithies, welding shops, secondhand clothes shops and junk shops, cart repair shops, Arab cafes, and close at hand—the abbattoir. On every side cries and shouts rose into the air, sounds of hammering and beating and thudding. Boys with sooty faces and blackened nails pounded with sledgehammers. Riva breathed in the air of the lively, dirty market with a sense of relief and strolled down the narrow street with the sewage water running slowly down the gutters on either side. When she reached the market she saw Hadassah standing next to the chicken slaughterer's and she quickly moved aside and hid, waiting for Hadassah to disappear from sight.

When she came home she opened all the windows and shutters, and the scents of the early spring filled the house. Weiss came home for lunch in a bad mood.

"I'm hungry as a dog. That Langfuss, it's hard work getting anything to the point out of him."

From the day he had risen from his mourning, Weiss had not shaved his beard. A strange piety had suddenly taken hold of him. He began getting up early in the morning to go

81

to the big synagogue. His piety increased to such an extent that all his acquaintances began to fear that his wife's death had unbalanced him. The girls were not yet accustomed to his bearded face, and in the colony people told all kinds of stories about the transformation that had taken place in him.

The new house was not easily found. Once more it seemed to the Weisses that they would never leave the house in Train Street. In her secret heart Riva was pleased.

· 13 ·

EVERYONE WANTED TO LIVE IN FOUNDERS STREET. NO ONE WHO already lived there wanted to move elsewhere. There was very little new building on the street, where the houses of the colony's rich were surrounded by gardens and ancient trees, as if they had been there forever. Even the omnipotent Langfuss, for all his energetic efforts, got nowhere.

Baruch was fading away. His eyes had the look of a hunted dog. Nechama found the axe he had hidden under his bed and was frightened out of her wits. Baruch almost stopped speaking. He had never been talkative, but now his silence was like a deliberate abstinence. When Nechama came and asked him about the axe, he jumped out of bed and brandished it at her. She ran out of the room shrieking and the axe remained with Baruch. She never tried to persuade him to give it to her again. Baruch's nights were troubled. Before dawn his eyes would fill with tears and the tears poured down his face. It was a wonder where Baruch got so many tears.

Weiss saw that the boy was ill and he forbade him to

work. "From now on you'll be an overseer like all the others," he said to him.

Baruch was ashamed to look Weiss in the eye or to thank him. His sufferings had endured for almost a year now, but there was still a flicker of life left in him, enough to give him the strength to continue the routine pattern of the life that had been laid down for him before he became conscious of his own desires.

He had almost forgotten the thing he had done in the field next to the citrus groves. The thoughts that filled his mind were worse than the act itself, and they were not even directly related to it. They grew and swelled out of all proportion. An inexplicable terror curdled his blood and he loathed himself and everyone related to him, including his mother. He felt no sorrow for what he had done or pity for the little girl who had made him do it. She was faceless, lifeless, nothing—a bundle of rags and the smell of dung and goat sweat in a summer field. But the sleepless nights, the anxiety of his mother tiptoeing about the house, visiting him in his sleep, eroded his spirit and made big, dark holes inside him.

The change in his employer's appearance, his gray beard and crumpled face, frightened Baruch, who imagined that nothing could be kept secret from Mr. Weiss and that the latter knew everything there was to know about him. Now he was more afraid than ever of meeting Weiss's eyes and talking to him. He interpreted every word that came out of Weiss's mouth as a command from on high and did whatever he was told like a person in a trance. He worked because he was bound to work and because work was the reason for his existence. When Weiss told him to stop working, he stopped although it upset him and wounded his pride. He walked about among the Arab workers, fed his donkey, and sat in the packing shed imagining ghastly scenes. And when the bell rang for the lunch break, he went pale and his throat tightened as if it were tolling for his death.

One evening when he came to Weiss's house he found him talking to Langfuss, and he got the idea into his head that they were plotting to fire him from his job as overseer. Weiss and Langfuss were sitting at the table and speaking in whispers, and Baruch sat on the bed and waited for his sentence to be passed. Finally Langfuss stood up, said goodbye, and left. Weiss rubbed the gray beard on his chin with his thumb and looked at Baruch as if he didn't know what to do with him.

"I'm better now, Mr. Weiss, I can work myself now," said Baruch although nobody had asked him.

"In any case there's not much work now," said Weiss.

Baruch lowered his eyes and mumbled, "It doesn't matter."

Weiss looked preoccupied and Baruch stood up to go, not wanting to disturb him. Weiss invited him to have something to drink, but Baruch was shy and his eyes begged to be let off this torture. Weiss could not understand Baruch's reluctance but he said goodbye and opened the door. He patted Baruch affectionately on the shoulder and Baruch mounted his donkey and disappeared from sight.

Weiss prepared himself to go to the synagogue and study with the old men. He called Riva and she brought him his supper, a mug of coffee and bread and jam.

"What does Langfuss say?"

"He's still looking," replied Weiss. "In the meantime, we'll stay in this hovel. If only we had moved into the new house before the summer at least . . ."

"We'll manage here too," said Riva.

"Where's Batsheva?" asked Weiss.

"Reading in our room."

AT TWILIGHT WEISS sat on the big veranda of the synagogue, with Shor the Monk at his side fulminating against the world—

denouncing the government and cursing the Jewish leadership for its passivity and obsequiousness, beside himself with rage at the treachery and disgrace, his eyes burning and his lips trembling. Shor the Monk's clothes were ragged, his wild red hair and beard obscured his face. Weiss did not reply, his heart was elsewhere, but the Monk's words did not disturb him, just as his own silence did not prevent the Monk from continuing his harangue. There was something about the Monk that made Weiss feel young again and gave him new strength. The Monk's words were cutting, violent; he shot them out like a fire shooting sparks, closing his eyes and brandishing his finger threateningly in the air.

On Fridays, before the Sabbath, the Monk patrolled the colony wailing like a siren with a whistle stuck in his mouth. The shopkeepers were afraid of him and immediately shut up their shops, because this Shor had a mean tongue, and he didn't keep his hands in his pockets either.

After the service they would sit at the back of the synagogue while the senile old rabbi expounded Talmudic texts to them. Shor would add lessons of his own drawn from the events of the times, and the uncomprehending rabbi would stare in bewilderment. They would try to shut Shor up and tell him not to interfere, but they could not curb his zeal. Lumping Weizmann together with the high commissioner, the underground movements with the police, and the workers with the farmers, he denounced and cursed them all with the passion of a prophet of wrath. Weiss gazed at him in astonishment and curiosity without understanding a word he said. When they celebrated the conclusion of a tractate of the Talmud, people brought cakes and drinks, but Shor the Monk touched neither food nor drink. His nervous, exquisitely beautiful hands writhed expectantly on his lap. What he was expecting, nobody knew.

The Monk lived alone in his hut. Weiss decided to invite

him for a Sabbath meal. At first the Monk refused, but in the end he succumbed to Weiss's blandishments and agreed to come.

When Batsheva heard that her father intended to bring Shor the Monk home to dinner, she announced that she for one would not sit down at the same table as that crazy beggar. Weiss was surprised and upset and he lost his temper. Riva was afraid that the evening would once again turn into a nightmare of hate.

Weiss controlled his anger and said calmly but furiously that he was still the master of the house and he would decide who to invite, and if Batsheva didn't like it, she had his permission to absent herself from the table.

"And you, Riva, will you stand and cook for that lunatic?" asked Batsheva.

"I'll hire a woman to do the work," said Weiss.

"Today is already Thursday," said Batsheva.

Riva sighed.

"I don't understand what's going on here," said Batsheva. "Everything is being turned upside down. Suddenly he's turned into a pious Jew. Going to pray in the synagogue two and three times a day. Growing a beard, making friends with beggars and madmen and inviting them home to meals. Why not invite Baruch too? He's been looking very poorly lately. And why not Masha at the same time? And the Arab workers too, why leave them out? We'll have a party for all the buffoons in town! And then he's surprised that we haven't got any friends among the farmers of the colony."

"Enough, Batsheva," pleaded Riva. "If he wants it so much, why shouldn't we do it for him?"

"You too! Everyone's going mad around us, Riva, we're sinking into an abyss. Perhaps mother cursed us, I don't know."

"Can't you see that she's insane? I'm telling you the girl

is mad," declared Weiss and rose from the table. "You can hear for yourself the kind of things she says."

Batsheva went pale with anger and her eyes opened very wide. Riva reflected that in the new house, if indeed they ever moved there, nothing would change. It would be better to get everything over here in Train Street, far away among the orange groves.

Weiss went outside and sat on the balustrade of the veranda in the dark. The trees that Baruch had planted had grown a little and the rhododendron bushes made clumsy shadows next to the fence. But now the trees and the bushes were no longer important, because they were going to move to a new house, in Founders Street. He waited outside for his temper to cool in the evening breeze and for Riva to calm Batsheva down. Weiss made up his mind to insist on having his own way.

All this time the teacher Borochov was sitting in the big room in Friedman's house. Friedman the drunk was already sleeping in his room. The approach of spring and summer always filled Borochov with the desire to do something, but he never knew what it was that he should do. Hadassah sat on the big armchair, ugly in her pregnancy, her once delicate face swollen and expressionless. Only her eyes still followed him caressingly, full of a boundless admiration. He felt out of place in the house. Outside was the silence of the night and inside—an oppressive weight. The weight of the sweet scent of the jasmine coming through the window, the drunken snores from the bedroom, and the endless, groundless expectation. Borochov stood up and walked about the room with Hadassah's eyes, kind and apologetic, following him. He went outside onto the veranda and into the dark garden, and Hadassah's eyes accompanied him like two faithful dogs. In the garden the air was shrill with crickets and heavy with the cloying scent of the jasmine bushes.

Not far from Friedman the drunk's house, Baruch lay open-eyed in his bed. His mother snored in her room, and the sound of her snores filled him with helpless rage and a desire to break something. He fingered the axe beneath his bed and the touch of the cold steel calmed him a little. A caravan of swarthy bedouin passed his window with their goods and chattels and their meager herds, which they were leading all the way to Egypt. Nomads with daggers hidden in their robes, their eyes clouded with blood and poison and their teeth as black as pitch. Their women were veiled and tattooed, and the chains of ancient silver coins wound about their necks and faces tinkled and rattled.

The nomads swarmed around the house, lighting fires. His donkey brayed from his stable and Baruch could not run to help him. They dragged his mother out bound hand and foot and lay her on the donkey's back. His poor old mother. Baruch was powerless to do anything, because everything was happening outside him, beyond his reach. He was transfixed, paralyzed, and dumb. The camels were grazing on his guava trees, which smelled like the smell of autumn. His mother did not cry; she lay still, crushed. He could not even stretch out his hand for his axe. The whole colony was sleeping and nobody heard a thing. Nobody knew. It was better that way. Everything was done in silence. The only sound was the rattling of the chains around the necks of the veiled women. The ropes cut deep lines in Nechama's old body, lines of blood, like the lines in the dry red summer soil, and she bumped up and down on the donkey's back.

The caravan disappeared into the darkness, on its way to Egypt. Everywhere they left behind them embers and dung, embers and dung. Baruch felt no sorrow, no fear or anger. Everything happened outside him. He could do nothing to save his kind, talkative old mother.

Baruch knew that it was nothing but the play of the shadows on his window. Not a dream, because he was wide awake and his eyes were open and very empty.

He could hear his mother snoring in her room. It was a kind of game brought by the night to put him to the test.

Weiss and Langfuss were plotting to get rid of him. The whole world had been turned upside down, as in an earthquake. The whole world, in one moment of madness and unconsciousness and living blood in the field. The Arab workers in the citrus grove too were plotting to take their revenge on him, they were conspiring against him. The summer was heavy from the start. Like a red hot stone pressing down from the sky. Outside the night was clear. Groups of girls from the training farm walked past in the street. The same girls, the same songs:

> And the girls who go down to the vineyards,
> And the girls who go down to the grape vines,
> Their eyes are as black as night . . .

Baruch jumped out of bed, brandished the axe, and closed the shutters with a bang. Then he went back to bed and covered his eyes with his two huge hands. When he opened his eyes for a second, he saw his mother standing at the foot of his bed staring at him in terror, like a shadow.

· 14 ·

SHOR THE MONK HAD BEEN INVITED TO EAT TWO MEALS AT THE Weiss home, Friday night dinner and Saturday lunch. Riva worked all day and night cooking her father's favorite dishes. The Yemenite maid cleaned and tidied the house.

"Anyone would think we were going to entertain the high commissioner himself," laughed Riva.

"Just don't mention his name to the Monk," said Weiss. "He hates him."

"I refuse to sit at the same table as that man," announced Batsheva again.

"I heard you the first time," said Weiss. "There's no need to repeat it every five minutes."

"Does Mr. Shor know how to use a knife and fork?" asked Batsheva.

"No, Batsheva. He eats with his hands, and sometimes with his feet too," said Weiss.

"You've got delightful friends, Father, I must say," retorted Batsheva in a sorrowful tone of voice.

Weiss stood up, took a change of clothing and a big towel, and went to bathe himself in the colony's *mikva*.

In the evening after the prayer service, Weiss and Shor the Monk walked down Train Street together. The table was laid in the big room with the Sabbath candles standing in the middle—Bracha Weiss's old silver candlesticks. Riva and Batsheva replied coldly to the merry cries of "Good Sabbath! Good Sabbath!" and after the men had washed their hands they all sat down at the table. Shor the Monk was wearing a filthy white shirt, his red hair surrounded his face like a halo of fire, and his little eyes blazed. Riva and Batsheva were silent throughout the meal, while their father conversed with the Monk. After the meal the two men broke into song, but the songs were savage, frightening roars, hoarse and ugly, not at all like the gentle Sabbath songs they were used to. Weiss tried to imitate his guest and even to outdo him in his yelling, and the girls stared at him in contempt. But he took no notice, and as if on purpose to annoy them he sang even louder than before and beamed at his guest with exaggerated hospitality. It was clear that he felt like a man released from a prison in which he had shut himself up of his own free will. Batsheva gave Riva a look that said as plainly as words, I told you so. Riva's face was flushed with affront and suppressed anger. She cleared the table with trembling hands and averted her eyes from her father. The Monk felt quite at home. He banged on the table in time to his peculiar singing until the cutlery and the candlesticks shook. When Weiss accompanied him to the outskirts of the colony after they had finished eating, his guest said, "I want you to know, Mr. Weiss, that you are one of the chosen few of this country. We are surrounded by thieves and cowards, sycophants, backbiters, and hired murderers. Eretz Israel won't tolerate them. It will spew them out and send them back to where they came from. Bolsheviks and Zionists and Revisionists, the whole pack of them, paid traitors every one."

Weiss made no reply, since he had already grown accustomed to hearing these arguments from his companion. Next to the railway line he offered the Monk his hand but Shor recoiled, shaking his head and waving his hands as if to say, no, no! and walked away.

When Weiss got back the table was already cleared. Riva and Batsheva were washing the dishes in the kitchen. To rebuke them for their lack of piety on the Sabbath, he went out to the porch and sat in the darkness. Batsheva came from the kitchen and deliberately switched on the light. Weiss opened his mouth to protest but shut it again without saying anything. Batsheva smiled and went back to the kitchen in triumph. He heard them whispering and he longed to know what they were talking about. The sense of her victory filled him with an oppressive emptiness and a feeling of bitter helplessness.

Finally he stood up and went to the kitchen door. "I see that Batsheva decided to honor our guest with her presence after all."

Batsheva did not respond to this provocation. She looked at him with cold, contemptuous eyes.

But Riva said, "You're making a fool of yourself, Father. Such men are not worthy of your friendship, they do not bring any honor to our home."

"What are you talking about, Riva? You don't understand. The man is a saint."

"Our father's sudden piety worries me," said Batsheva.

"I didn't ask for your opinion," said Weiss.

"He's going out of his mind, Riva, he's losing his wits."

Weiss smiled a bitter, superior smile. "You think I haven't heard you talking in your room at night? I can hear everything. I don't care. Let the whole world come and shout in my ear that I've gone mad, I won't budge an inch. But you two will have to respect my wishes and observe the Sabbath. I won't stand for provocations in my own house. Good night."

THE LANGFUSS HOME was opposite the big synagogue, and the Langfusses had grown so used to the noise of the praying over the years that they no longer heard it.

"The older ignoramuses like Weiss grow, the crazier they get," said Langfuss to his widowed mother, who shrugged her shoulders and sighed.

"He wants two kitchen sinks in his new house," said the broker. "One for meat and one for milk dishes. Where am I going to find him a house like that in Founders Street? He's prepared to sell a grove he bought from me only last year."

"Never mind," said the widow Langfuss. "Between the buying and the selling something comes your way, and that's the main thing."

Moishe Langfuss grabbed his mother round the waist and began dancing madly with her up and down the room. His mother shrieked and begged him to stop, because everybody could see them from the street. But her son refused to stop his romping. The midday Sabbath sun flooded the dark-walled room. The table was covered with a green velvet cloth and the beads on its fringes glittered like drops of clear water. Heavy black furniture filled the room and made it dark and solemn. Moishe Langfuss kept whispering nonsense into his mother's big ears until the old woman was weak with laughter.

The widow Langfuss spent most of her time next to the window, watching to see who went by in the main street of the colony. "Come and see, Moishe," she called, standing by the window to get her breath.

Langfuss came and stood next to her and saw Haim Weiss strolling down the street with Shor the Monk. He sighed and smiled wryly. Then he left the window and lay down on the couch and began to read the newspapers piled on the floor next to it.

Weiss walked down the street with the Monk, and when they crossed the railway tracks he told him that he intended moving into a new house in Founders Street, where he would have two kitchen sinks, one for meat dishes and one for milk. These words did not appear to make a great impression on the Monk, for he said nothing, but his eyes blazed.

When they entered the house the girls once more received them coldly. They sat down at the table and blessed the wine and the bread. After the soup and the fish Riva brought a roast to the table. Shor put a piece of meat to his mouth and suddenly he screamed. His face paled, his eyes opened wide, and his arms flailed about as if he were drowning. He spat the meat out onto his plate and began to shriek, "Blood! Blood! Carrion flesh! Raw meat! Idolatry! Living blood!"

Riva was petrified with offense and alarm, Weiss buried his face in his hands. The Monk got up from the table and began jumping around the room as if his feet were on fire. Batsheva stood up calmly, cool and composed, pointed to the passage door, and said, "Out, Mr. Shor! Get out at once!"

Shor the Monk did not leave. He went on capering about the room, clapping his hands and mumbling indistinctly, until finally he stood still and announced that they wanted to poison him. Weiss raised his head and said, "Please leave, Mr. Shor."

Shor was not put out. He strode calmly to the passage and stood in the doorway. He spat, cursed, and left the house, slamming the door behind him.

The three Weisses went on sitting in silence until Batsheva said, "Are you sorry now, Father? Was it worth it?"

"Shut up, you bitch," said Weiss in a strangled voice, and his eyes misted over.

Riva suddenly broke her silence with a shriek, "Enough! I can't stand it any more!"

She was crying and laughing at once. Her father stood up and slapped her on both cheeks. Her eyes rolled up and she fell silent. She went into the kitchen and washed her face and wet her hair. Then she returned to the room and began silently to collect the plates. Weiss went up to her and embraced her. He pressed her to his chest, stroked her wet hair with his other hand, and whispered, "My poor good little Riva. What's happening to us?"

Batsheva looked at them frowning and pleating the white tablecloth nervously between her fingers. Then she stood up and cleared away the remaining dishes. Riva extricated herself from her father's embrace and ran to her room. Her sister stood in the kitchen and washed the dishes. Weiss came and asked her if he could help.

"What is Riva doing?" asked Batsheva.

"She's lying in bed shivering," he replied.

"Exactly like Mother," sighed Batsheva.

"Like Mother," said Weiss after a moment's silence. "This evening I'll go to Langfuss. We have to make him hurry up with the new house. He's taking his time deliberately in order to squeeze more money out of me."

After the Sabbath Weiss went to Langfuss's house on his way home from the synagogue. He knocked on the door. There was no reply. The house was dark and closed, as if its owners had gone away on a long journey. Weiss was alarmed and he decided to sit on the steps and wait for them to come back, either the son or his mother. He did not know how much time had passed when someone suddenly shook him by the shoulder. When he looked up he saw Langfuss and his mother standing in astonishment at the bottom of the steps.

"I wasn't feeling well," said Weiss. "I sat down to rest for a moment and I fell asleep."

"Perhaps you should come in for a moment and have something to drink," said the widow Langfuss anxiously.

Weiss stood up immediately, blurted out thanks and goodbye, and walked away. Langfuss and his mother shook their heads, sighed, and smiled sorrowfully. Weiss thought that they were looking at him as if he were mad. He hastened his pace and hurried home in a state of confusion. When he arrived he found Riva asleep.

"How does she feel?" he asked Batsheva.

"I was worried about you, Father. What kept you until now? It's very late."

"How's Riva?"

"Riva feels fine. I think she was putting on a bit of an act this afternoon. Poor girl."

Weiss did not reply. He went straight to bed and put out the light.

· 15 ·

THE TEACHER BOROCHOV TOO HAD PUT ON WEIGHT SINCE HIS marriage. He had grown a double chin on his round pink face, and his body had grown heavy and clumsy. His new life bored him, and he didn't know why. Most evenings Friedman would come home drunk and sing his silly songs. Hadassah, in her last months of pregnancy, would sit and look at Borochov expectantly; the long vacation had come round again and there wasn't much work at the cultural committee.

One evening he went out without saying anything. He walked about the streets of the colony with downcast eyes and his hands in his pockets, as if he were looking for something. His feet carried him to the cultural committee hut. There was a light on in the hut and a few people were sitting reading the newspapers. He went in and greeted them. Then he went out again and walked to Founders Street. He reached the water tower hill and saw couples walking arm in arm, sitting and embracing on the benches, giggling and enjoying themselves, and his heart nearly broke. If only he were a poet, he thought regretfully, if only he could find words for the melody singing in his heart and choking up his throat. Even the scent of the gardens no longer moved him. He did not know if the scents had changed or if he was perhaps growing immune to them.

Suddenly he found himself in the big synagogue square, standing opposite Langfuss's house, where he saw Langfuss and his mother sitting and talking to Weiss and Riva in the window of the brightly lit room. Batsheva was not with them. He lingered there for a while and understood that they were talking about the new house in Founders Street and that they were already discussing concrete details. Up to now he had imagined that it was nothing but a rumor, simply a fantasy on the part of Haim Weiss.

He hurried away and arrived at the big marketplace. The market was dark and locked. Like a market in a little Jewish *shtetl* in the Diaspora, he said to himself, stroking the walls of the shops and the empty stalls, running his fingers distractedly over the bars.

Suddenly he was in Train Street with his feet bearing him in the direction of the railway tracks. After he had crossed the tracks, he strode up the dirt road to Haim Weiss's house. He stood for a moment by the door. He could hear Batsheva singing inside and the sound of water splashing in the bathroom.

When he heard her coming out of the bathroom, he knocked. Batsheva came to the door and asked nervously, "Who's there?"

"It's me," he said, "Borochov."

"Borochov? What's the matter? Has anything happened?"

He did not reply. He waited for her to open the door. The door opened a crack and her head peeped out. When she saw his face she opened the door. He hung back on the threshold, as if he was unwilling to enter.

"Come inside before I catch cold," she said, and her voice was warm and soft.

He went in and looked at her. She was wearing a toweling robe with a blue checked pattern, blue like her eyes, and her hair was wet and gathered on the nape of her neck. A bitter, intoxicating smell of almond soap rose from her body and enflamed his senses. Her face was smooth and shining.

He followed her into the big room, without knowing how he would explain his visit. She excused herself and turned away to go to her room and get dressed, but suddenly he rose and seized her hand.

"No, Batsheva."

She was astonished. Her eyes opened wide under her black,

still wet lashes, and her breast began rising and falling rapidly underneath her robe. The teacher Borochov closed his eyes and embraced her tightly. She tried to free herself from his embrace, but there was enormous strength in his arms. He bent over her mouth and began loosening her robe. She pulled him into her room and there, next to the door, his mouth groped for her lips as he murmured, "Batsheva, my simple little Batsheva," his voice close to tears, "my good, gentle Batsheva."

"MOTHER, SIT UP with me all night," Baruch pleaded with his mother. "I'm afraid, I'm terribly afraid."

His mother looked at him in alarm. "Perhaps I should call the doctor," she implored.

"No doctor and no nothing," said Baruch. "I'm afraid, that's all. I can't sleep at night because I'm so frightened."

"I've never heard you talk like this before," protested his mother.

"They're going to kill me, Mother. That's all. Now I know that I'm afraid. Before I thought that I wasn't afraid. I don't know anything, but I'm afraid."

"So that's why you keep the axe under your bed."

"What did you think?"

"I didn't know."

"That I wanted to kill you?"

"God forbid, Baruch. You're not normal."

"That's it, Mother, I'm not normal," said Baruch, and he burst into tears. His mother thought that perhaps he was drunk. She drew closer to smell his breath. His mouth stank as usual. All year long she had known that there was something wrong with Baruch, but he had suppressed his weeping at night so that she would not hear. Now he felt the need to cry in front of her. Nechama had not seen Baruch cry since he was a baby. Even when his father died, when he was twenty-five or more, he had not shed a single tear, not even in the cemetery.

"You must be in love," his mother comforted him.

"Go to hell, you and your jokes. It's all your fault."

"Baruch!" cried Nechama, as if she had suddenly made a terrible discovery, "you're mad!"

"You're a strong woman, Mother," wept Baruch. "Stronger than steel, God bless you."

"A year ago already, when you shut yourself in the bathroom and you wouldn't come out, I thought you were mad, but I was afraid to tell you. I thought you would kill me."

"Sit next to me and shut up," commanded Baruch quietly.

The tears welled out of the slits of his little eyes and collected next to his nose and in the corners of his mouth, and from there they dripped onto his chin and his throat. He didn't even wipe them away.

"It's because you don't go out with girls, that's your trouble," stated his mother. "It blocks up your blood vessels and drives you mad. How can you live like this at all?"

She sat next to him all night and waited until he fell asleep.

THEY MIGHT COME back at any moment! The teacher Borochov suddenly shuddered and turned pale. Batsheva raised herself on her elbows. Her blue eyes were cold and empty and her lips were white.

He stood up and got dressed in panic-stricken haste, and she watched him with open disgust. The pink fat and the smooth self-satisfaction that, despite his sudden panic, still shone from his face, aroused a violent hostility in her. She wrapped herself tightly in her bathrobe and went laboriously to the bathroom. He heard the bathroom door close and the splash of the water, and he hurried from the house. On the dirt road he made out the shadows of Weiss and Riva and heard their voices. They were crossing the railway tracks.

He crouched down next to one of the irrigation trenches and washed his face. He saw them going into the house. He stood up, smoothed his wet hair back, tidied his crumpled clothes, and walked away wringing his hands and saying to himself, "I'll never forgive myself . . . I'll never forgive myself . . ."

He reached his sleeping street and saw that the light was still on in his bedroom. He did not dare to go in and went on walking down the street. Next to Nechama's house he sat down on the bench which was damp with dew and decided to rest for a while.

Suddenly he heard the sound of weeping. Baruch groaned, and his mother soothed him and said, "Enough, Baruch, it's late already. Go to sleep. Tomorrow you have to go to work. I'm here next to you all the time, don't be afraid."

"They're going to kill me," wept Baruch.

The teacher Borochov's hair stood on end with fear. He rose immediately to his feet and tiptoed home.

"This summer is driving people out of their minds," he said to himself. "After her father dies we'll sell the house and move to the Galilee or to Jerusalem."

Hadassah was still awake, waiting up for him, and he hugged and kissed her instead of answering her questions. His wife lay next to him with his son breathing inside her belly. All the tormenting thoughts left him immediately. It seemed to him that he and Hadassah had been lying side by side like this for days, and everything else was as remote and fantastic as a nightmare.

· 16 ·

LANGFUSS FOUND A HOUSE FOR WEISS IN FOUNDERS STREET. THE
house did not have two sinks in its kitchen, but they could
always install an additional sink. The house stood not far
from the water tower hill, and the price was very high. It
was a large house with many rooms. There was a well-
tended garden in front and a little orchard in the back with
various fruit trees, tall and already producing fruit. Weiss
conducted lengthy arguments with Langfuss about the
price, and it became clear to him that the price he would
get for his grove would not be enough for half the new
house.

Langfuss saw that the idea of the new house in Founders
Street had fixed itself firmly in Weiss's mind, and he realized
that the old man would pay any price he had to in the end.

"Look at the walls," demanded Weiss. "They're as thin
as paper! Is this the modern building you were talking about?
Why, you could bore a hole in them with a pin!"

Langfuss looked at him with a patronizing smile. "That's
the way they build nowadays, Mr. Weiss," he said. "Today
there are new materials for building. There's no need for
thick walls."

This explanation did not satisfy Weiss, but he went on
visiting the house. The pale little woman who opened the
door shut herself into one of the rooms with her husband
and allowed them to roam freely over the house.

"Porcelain, all real porcelain, Mr. Weiss," said Langfuss,
tapping his finger like an expert on the white tiles in the
bathroom and cupping his ear to hear the sound made by
his taps—the proof of the high quality of the tiles.

A real estate broker's comedy, reflected Weiss, and took
no notice of Langfuss's antics.

"So," he said, "it's modern, is it? That's the way it's supposed to be."

"And a separate lavatory, inside the house," said Langfuss enthusiastically, laying one hand on Weiss's shoulder while pointing with the other down the long passage.

"All right, all right," said Weiss shortly, and refused to go any farther. "It will be hot here in summer," he added after a silence. "The roof is flat, without tiles."

"You're mistaken, Mr. Weiss, you're mistaken," protested Langfuss, expressing indignation with all his short fat body, while his hands set out to fight the battle for truth on the old man's sleeves. "Greatly mistaken. Tiled roofs are not modern. Modern engineering has discovered the existence of what is called a vacuum between the tiled roof and the ceiling of the house. The vacuum heats up gradually and cools down slowly. All day long it heats up and at night it gives off the heat. Into the house. A flat roof cools down in a jiffy. In the afternoon the sun moves away a little and already the house is cool and chilly. Not to speak of the night—not to mention the fact that both big rooms have three windows, and the other rooms have at least two, and consequently the cross ventilation . . ."

In the afternoon, after Batsheva came home from work, the three of them went to visit the house in Founders Street. The little woman opened the door without looking at them. Her husband called her immediately from the room and she obeyed his call, allowing them to roam the house as freely as if they were in their own house. Haim Weiss and his daughters walked on tiptoe and spoke in whispers. The house was grand and spacious. Its furniture was dark and heavy, soft thick carpets were spread on the floors. The windows were large and overlooked shady trees in the garden and the curtains fluttered in every light breeze. Riva and Batsheva walked through the rooms as if they were in an enchanted palace. Weiss smiled as them with a triumphant, proprietary expression.

Suddenly the little woman popped out and whispered in his ear, "He'll sell you the furniture and the carpets too," and she pointed in the direction of the room where her husband was sitting, smiled, and scurried off before they had a chance to question her.

Batsheva looked at her father imploringly. Their own furniture was old and shabby and would not go far in a house this size. Weiss said nothing, but it was evident from his narrowed eyes and frowning brow that he suspected something.

Riva asked what they needed such a big house and so many rooms for. Batsheva stared at her angrily.

"The whitewash is fresh on the walls," said Weiss. "I don't like it."

"On the contrary," remarked Batsheva, "I think it's very nice."

Weiss decided to buy the house with the furniture and everything in it. He was already losing count in his head of the money he would need. He urged the girls to conclude the visit. When they left the house and started walking down the garden path, shady in the gloaming, his two daughters seemed to him to be lost in a dream.

For the time being they had no buyers for the house in Train Street. Langfuss claimed that these days nobody wanted to live outside the colony because of the danger from the Arabs. He suggested looking for people to rent the house instead of buying it. This being the case, Weiss was obliged to sell another grove and he was thus left with only one grove, Levin's grove, his first big citrus grove. His ready cash was dwindling fast.

He said to his daughters, "Now you will be able to bring your young men home at last." The girls said nothing.

"What do you think, that I've spent so much money for myself? I've already been married! How long am I going to go on having you on my hands?"

"In that case, why didn't you buy two houses?"

"We have two houses, my dear. We're not going to sell this house. We're going to rent it."

Riva tried to change the subject but Batsheva took no notice of her.

"Wait a minute, Riva," said Weiss, "your sister wants to say something interesting."

"I want to know your plans," said Batsheva.

"My plans?" asked Weiss. "Very simple. Whichever one of you marries first will get the house in Founders Street. The other will have to make do with this one. First come, first served."

"Like a lottery."

"What did you imagine?" said Weiss. "That life is any better or fairer than a lottery? Neither of you lives in the real world, my dears. You're a pair of babies."

They sat in the big room and no one thought about supper. Riva lay with her legs crossed on the couch. Batsheva sat opposite her on the armchair, and Weiss sat in his customary chair at the head of the table.

"You'll need somebody to protect you after I'm dead. Girls can't survive on their own."

"I have a steady job," said Batsheva. "I'm not afraid. I'll get married when I want to, to the man of my choice."

"Who said anything else?" cried Weiss. "Did I tell you to rush outside and drag the first man you meet by his hair to the rabbi? But you should try to hurry things up a little. It seems to me that neither of you is even thinking in that direction—that you want to go on living in the paradise of childhood forever."

"All this business of the new house, first come, first served, and so on—you understand, don't you, Riva? He wants to

104

set us against each other. That's all. Or perhaps he has something else in mind that I don't know about.''

"I said long ago that this house is quite good enough for me," said Riva.

"Langfuss says that it's dangerous to live outside the colony now," Weiss said. "The Arabs are making trouble and soon they'll be making pogroms. The first houses to suffer will be the ones outside the colony—the isolated ones."

"You don't seem afraid," said Batsheva.

"I place my faith in Divine Providence."

Batsheva laughed. "And where will you live?" she asked.

"You're not married yet, so the question is hypothetical."

"And nevertheless—if we both got married?"

"I'd manage."

"How?"

"Don't worry, Batsheva, I won't be a burden on you," he said bitterly.

"God forbid, Father," said Riva. "I can't understand what you're getting at, Batsheva."

"You're always backward," replied Batsheva. "He's making a deal with us, with conditions, which means that we have to know everything down to the last detail. And I don't know everything yet. He's hiding something from us."

"I'm not hiding anything."

"If not, why don't you answer my question?"

"What is your question?"

"Where will you live after we're both married?"

"I told you. That question is still hypothetical, unfortunately. But if you must know, let me tell you that I've still got enough money left to buy myself a room, or even a small apartment."

This answer did not completely satisfy Batsheva, but she asked no more questions.

Riva suddenly jumped off the couch. "What about supper?"

Nobody answered. They had lost their appetites. Riva understood and lay down again.

Weiss sat thinking and suddenly he said, "After you're married, perhaps I'll get married again too, so as not to be a millstone around your necks."

· 17 ·

THE GIRLS WERE TOO ASTONISHED TO SPEAK. WEISS LOOKED AT them and smiled to himself. Riva bristled with outrage. Finally she said, "What are you talking about, Father? It goes without saying that we will take care of all your needs. And by the way, you're not so old that you're in danger of being a burden on anyone."

"You don't understand, Riva," said Batsheva. "That's what it's all about. He's trying to prepare us for his remarriage. That's the whole thing in a nutshell. That's what's behind all this talk about the new house, and first come, first served, and the millstone around our necks. It's all clear to me now."

"How do you know what my intentions are?" asked Weiss angrily. Then he calmed down and said, "I told you I would do it, if at all, only after you're both married."

"The season of love is here," sang Batsheva, nodding her head at him as if she were humoring a lunatic.

Weiss kept his temper and did not stand on his dignity as the father and head of the house, wanting to prevent the storm he saw brewing in Batsheva, whose flashing eyes were sending out danger signals. He decided that this time he would not give her the satisfaction of reacting to her wounding barbs.

Riva looked at her sister and made a remark about Borochov. Batsheva imagined that Riva knew everything. Batsheva's nights were full of fantasies. The picture of Borochov grew blurred and disintegrated. In the end she was unable to distinguish between fact and fantasy, and the suspicion even entered her heart that the whole thing was a nightmare or a delusion, the fruit of her wishes or her fears.

Whenever Riva mentioned the teacher Borochov's name, Batsheva again imagined from the look in her sister's eyes that she knew the whole truth. Then the pieces fell into place again, and the picture rose before her eyes, free of the dross of imagination and panic, as the truth.

"Why are you looking at me like that? Is it my fault that you didn't listen to Mother's advice to make friends with the teacher Borochov?"

"I know that you detest him, Batsheva, but I don't know why."

"You're going to blame me for robbing you of your happiness for the rest of your life, aren't you? You don't say much but you know how to put on the airs of a martyr, just like Mother."

"Are you starting again?" shouted Weiss. "I don't want to hear anything more about it!"

"Even if I had agreed to Mother's request," said Riva with a smile, "he was already attached to Hadassah Friedman. They got married soon afterward."

"What do I care about all that?" exclaimed Batsheva angrily. "What do I care about that stupid Hadassah Friedman with her stricken calf's eyes and her drunken father and her marriage? What do you want of my life?"

"What do we want of your life?" asked Weiss.

"You're tired, Batsheva. You're depressed. I'll make up your bed," said Riva.

"It's early," said Batsheva. Her triangular face hardened and her eyebrows arched above the cold blue of her eyes.

"Aren't you hungry?" asked Riva.

"Stop looking at me as if I were sick. I don't need your help."

"Batsheva . . ."

"The pair of you drove Mother crazy and you buried her. You won't succeed with me," said Batsheva.

Weiss jumped up, his lips pale and his face red with rage. "You dare to talk, Batsheva? All this time I've kept quiet and buried the pain inside me in order not to make trouble in the home. You blame me? Us? Our Riva? It was you who killed your mother, with your own hands, with your own wicked mouth! She's tearing her to pieces! She's tearing her to pieces! I would cry in my heart when I saw you tormenting her. I know only too well what I can expect from you, or perhaps from the pair of you together, because Riva's good natured but she's got no character, she's under your thumb. I've never raised my hand against anyone, never mind my own daughters, not even when you were little girls. But I'd like to give you a good slap in the face now for your insolence, for your brazen cheek!"

"Please, Father, go ahead," said Batsheva, offering her cheek, "if it eases your conscience and your feelings of guilt."

Riva stood up breathing heavily and turned to go to her room, but she suddenly felt afraid that they might make it up in her absence. She stopped and turned to face them, leaning against the doorpost.

"Now he's trying to set us against each other," said Batsheva, looking at Riva. "To drag Mother into it and desecrate her memory, all for the sake of a house in Founders Street."

"It's late, Batsheva," begged Riva, "we should go to bed."

"It's ten to eight, to be precise," said Weiss. "The days are getting shorter and it gets dark early."

At that moment there was a knock at the door. They were too astonished to move.

Batsheva, full of forebodings, got up at once and shut herself in her room. Weiss went to open the door. It was

Langfuss, and in a little group behind him were Masha's mother, the chicken plucker from the market, Masha's skinny father, pale and unshaven, and Masha herself, wearing one of her brightly colored dresses and smelling strongly of scent.

Weiss asked them in and looked inquiringly at Langfuss. Langfuss explained politely that the lady and gentleman, Masha's parents ("Hershkovitz," corrected Masha's father), Mr. and Mrs. Hershkovitz, that is, wanted to see the house with a view to renting it if they found it to their satisfaction.

"With pleasure, with pleasure," said Weiss, and with obvious distaste shook the thin white hands of the out-of-work man and his chicken-plucking wife. Then he pushed his hands into his pockets and rubbed them against the lining. He showed them into the big room, and Masha's mother's face shone with excitement and sorrow. They walked through the room with its peeling walls and the late Bracha's sooty little kitchen, and crossed the wooden floorboards of the corridor with dreamy expressions on their faces. Riva reflected that they themselves must have looked exactly the same on the day they went to look at the little woman's house in Founders Street. Masha's mother smiled at Riva sadly, as if she were apologizing for something, and Mr. Hershkovitz poked her with his elbow to hurry her up.

Masha examined every corner inquisitively and said to Langfuss, "We're leaving a good house because of the troubles, and you bring us to see a house right outside the colony. What's the point?"

Langfuss was not put out. "Miss Masha, what are you talking about? There are no Arab villages in this direction. Only the workers in the citrus groves, and they would be the last to start any trouble. The house you're living in now is ten minutes away from the Arab village!"

"Really, Mr. Langfuss, you must think I was born on the moon! Why, exactly here, just behind Mr. Levin's orange grove . . ."

"Hold your tongue!" commanded Masha's father. "Don't take any notice of her, Mr. Langfuss."

"What's come over you, Masha, how can you speak like that to Mr. Langfuss?" said her mother.

"No, no." Langfuss came to Masha's aid. "She's quite right to ask questions. Everything must be clarified in advance, before it's too late . . ."

"What do you want of the girl, Yehezkiel?" said Masha's mother. "You see, she's quite right."

"She shouldn't interfere at all," said Mr. Hershkovitz. "Nobody asked for her opinion."

When Batsheva returned to the living room, the sisters forgot everything; their shoulders shook with suppressed laughter. Masha noticed and blushed to the roots of her hair. Her spirits fell and she leaned against the doorpost and said no more. Langfuss seized Weiss by the arm and gave him an encouraging squeeze. Weiss pretended not to take the hint and looked at his guests with tired disinterest when their tour of inspection of the little house was over. Masha's father pushed his wife to speak first. Mrs. Hershkovitz was a fat woman with a kerchief tied permanently around her gray hair and a perpetual smile in her sad, watery eyes.

"Mr. Weiss," she said, "we have nothing to hide from you. We are not wealthy people. My husband is a sick man, always out of work, but I myself work, and our Masha too, and we have managed to save a little money, not enough to buy a house of our own, but at least to move into a better house for rent. Up to now we have been living in an old packing shed . . ."

Here her husband cut in with the remark that there was no need to begin from prehistory, as they were disturbing the owner of the house.

The owner of the house protested that they were not disturbing him at all and asked them to sit down. They refused and went on standing in order not to be in anybody's way, and Masha's mother continued. "We have nothing to hide from you, Mr. Weiss . . ."

"You've said that already," grumbled her husband, blinking his eyes in irritation.

Mrs. Hershkovitz's voice began to quaver and her eyes softened, opened wide, and then narrowed. "We like your house. We are a large family with a lot of children, may God keep them healthy, and we have never taken a penny from anyone. We've always managed on what we had, worked hard, and never fallen into debt. We've never asked for help from anyone, not even when the children were sick and hungry . . ."

Here big tears began to pour from her eyes, and the corners of her mouth twitched convulsively. She took out a big man's handkerchief and wiped her eyes before continuing. "Your relative, Mr. Borochov," she sobbed, "knows us and our story . . ."

Her husband blinked and quivered with fury.

Masha decided to come to the point. "How much will it come to?" she asked. "The key money and the rent?"

Langfuss waved his open hand and said that it was too early to go into details. He had only brought them to show them the house and hear how they liked it. Money was a separate matter.

"Of course," said Masha's father, and looked contemptuously at Masha and her mother, who was wiping her eyes and blowing her nose with the large man's handkerchief. "Of course, nobody does business in such a hurry."

Langfuss shepherded them out to the corridor, conferred with them in whispers, opened the door for them, and immediately shut it behind them. When he returned to the room he found Weiss sitting deep in thought and the two girls standing expectantly at the door.

"You close the deal with them," requested Weiss. "Whatever you think is fair. I can't bargain with them."

"Bargaining is *my* profession," laughed Langfuss heartily. He settled down comfortably in the armchair, crossed his legs, scratched his little mustache with his thumbnail, and removed his spectacles and began to polish them. "That's what I get paid for!"

"Mr. Langfuss, won't you have supper with us?" asked Riva. "Please."

Langfuss immediately took his hat and rose to his feet. "No, no. Forgive me. I wouldn't dream of disturbing you."

"You're not disturbing us," said Weiss flatly. "You're being asked to have something to eat, so eat. We're not going to kill the fatted goose for you."

Langfuss was embarrassed, and Riva pressed him, "Please, Mr. Langfuss, why won't you stay and have supper with us?"

Langfuss saw that he would not be able to refuse and returned to the armchair.

"How is your mother?" asked Batsheva with cold politeness.

"Well, thank you, Batsheva," he replied, "and how are you?"

"Thank you."

"And the work at the bank?"

"Boring as usual," smiled Batsheva.

"What did you think? That you were going to run the economy of the Yishuv?" said Langfuss apologetically.

"God forbid. I'm not complaining."

Riva came back and laid the table. Langfuss saw that she was looking at him tenderly, and he was embarrassed.

"How will you have your egg, Mr. Langfuss?"

"Like everybody else," he sighed, "like everybody else. Whatever is the least trouble."

"It's all the same," smiled Riva. "There's no difference."

"Like everybody else," insisted the broker.

Riva went back to the kitchen and Batsheva said, "I'm dying to move into the new house already."

"You'll be able to move in at the end of the week. The people are moving out within the next few days."

"Our father has prepared a surprise for us," said Batsheva. "You know: Whichever of us marries first will get the new house. The other will have to be content with this one."

The startled Langfuss began to giggle to hide his embarrassment.

"Batsheva and her sense of humor," he smiled and winked at Weiss.

Riva stopped clattering dishes in the kitchen so that she would be able to hear every word.

"No, seriously," continued Batsheva. "He also told us that he intends getting married again himself. We will all get married and the world will be full of happiness."

In the kitchen Riva closed her eyes and her head spun.

"How much do you think I'll get from them in key money?" Weiss cut in.

"We'll have to wait and see," sighed Langfuss, clasping his hands together. "I can't promise anything yet, not until I've negotiated with them."

"In the end he himself will be without a home," said Batsheva. "Because he's dividing the two houses between the two of us. And he doesn't want to be a millstone round our necks, or so he says."

Riva dropped a plate in the kitchen and smashed it to smithereens.

"But you should know, Mr. Weiss," continued Langfuss, taking no notice of Batsheva, "that nowadays when a man rents a house he can't get the occupants out so easily. You can't force the tenants to vacate."

"Perhaps he'll marry a rich woman," said Batsheva, "and she will provide him with a better house than both our houses put together. A rich woman, maybe young and beautiful too, not like our mother who died of overwork."

Riva came in and began to serve the food. She sat down in her place and said, "Bon appetit."

No one started eating. Each was waiting for someone else to begin.

"Why aren't you eating," asked Riva, her voice close to tears.

Weiss stuck his fork into his food first and began eating slowly and without relish. The others joined in silently. Riva thought that her sister was preparing additional remarks, and she kept looking at her out of the corner of her eye. But Batsheva ate with a pensive expression on her face, as if there were nobody else in the room. Langfuss ate unwillingly, chewing the pieces of omelette and shreds of vegetables with evident distaste.

Weiss asked him, "What is all this talk of Arab rioting and marauders? Another *Galuth* in the offing?"

"I told you it would be better for you to live inside the colony now," replied the broker.

"But what about the orange groves?" asked Weiss anxiously.

"I wouldn't walk around there at night," said Langfuss.

"I can't visit my own groves when I feel like it?"

"Go and complain to the Arabs," said Batsheva. "Explain to them, perhaps they'll understand."

"My workers are perfectly all right," said Weiss. "My Baruch knows them."

Riva served coffee and cake. Langfuss refused a slice of cake; he felt that another bite would make him sick. Riva looked at him imploringly. "Please take a piece of cake, Mr. Langfuss. I made it myself."

"Take!" commanded Weiss. "She made it herself, with all her heart."

Langfuss took a piece of cake and bit into it. The cake was

sweet and rich and he could not swallow it. He praised its taste, chewed lengthily, and forced himself to swallow. Then he lit a fragrant cigarette and inhaled deeply, to get rid of the oily sweet taste of the cake. Riva cleared the dishes off the table and went into the kitchen. She remained there for a long time, and when she returned to the room she was dressed and her hair was combed as if she was going out.

"Where are you going?" asked Batsheva in surprise.

"None of your business!" exclaimed Weiss angrily.

"Allow me to accompany you, Riva," said Langfuss.

Batsheva said nothing. She picked up her book and began to read. Riva and Langfuss took their leave and went out.

Outside the night was chilly. Riva prayed for Langfuss to say something to her. They walked slowly down the dirt road and the orange groves all around them cast dark shadows on the path.

"To tell the truth," said Riva with a smile, "I'm a little frightened. After all you said."

"There's nothing to be afraid of," said Langfuss in a wise voice. "Whatever will be will be, irrespective of circumstances."

"Do you believe in fate, Mr. Langfuss?"

"Yes, Riva," said Langfuss. "There's no getting away from it."

"And do you believe in God?"

"There are things that are beyond our understanding," he said.

"My father has suddenly become orthodox since my mother's death. Batsheva says that it isn't normal."

"It happens to many people when they reach a certain age and begin to worry about the approaching end. They think, what if there's something in all those religious beliefs about the world to come, and they try to change their ways before it's too late. What have they got to lose? If it doesn't do any good, at least it can't do any harm."

Riva smiled in embarrassment and prayed silently that they would not reach the colony too quickly and he would not ask her where she was going. He was not shorter than she was, as she had always imagined owing to the width of his body. His appearance was pleasant, his voice gentle and wise, a little on the loud side. She hoped fervently that he would say something nice to her, something that would warm her heart.

"What's happening to Batsheva?" he suddenly asked as they crossed the railway tracks.

"She's suffering," sighed Riva. "Something is troubling her, eating her up inside." She longed to make a clean breast of everything, to take him into her confidence. "She's mentally ill. It's impossible to live with her. She destroys everything with her tongue. She's shortening Father's life."

She wanted to tell him about her mother, but she choked on the words and couldn't go on.

Langfuss walked by her side, keeping a short distance between them. He did not look directly at her. She wanted to feel the touch of his hand on her arm, but he maintained his distance. Her nerves were stretched to breaking point and she was afraid that she would do something that would bring a dreadful disgrace down on her head. The central marketplace was already looming before them and she still didn't know what she would say when he asked her where she wanted to go.

Close to the big synagogue she offered him her hand in parting. She longed to feel the warmth of his palm. But he quickly took it back again and smiled at her with maddening politeness. When she left him she regretted the things she had said about Batsheva. She realized that she had taken leave of her senses and lost control of her tongue. She intended walking down Founders Street as far as the water tower hill, but suddenly she remembered that Batsheva was alone with her father in the house. She turned on her tracks, and she began to see Arab marauders slipping out of the shadows in the marketplace and dogging her footsteps. She remembered her mother and her nightmare fears of the murderers. She broke into a terrified run, crossed the railway tracks, and heard rustling and wailing noises encroaching on her from the citrus groves as she ran. When she arrived at home she stood panting at the door for a few moments and put her ear to the keyhole. But the house was still, in spite of the fact that the lights were on in the rooms. "They've made up," she thought angrily. She went in and avoided her father's eyes. Batsheva was lying on her bed fully clothed, weeping softly.

Riva was afraid that she was going to collapse. She sat on her sister's bed and looked at her helplessly. Batsheva appeared not to notice her. It was the first time Riva had ever seen her cry.

She bent over her and looked into her eyes to make her recognize her. "What's the matter?" she asked. "What's the matter, Batsheva?"

"He called you a whore."

"Who?"

"Father."

"Me?"

"Yes."

"Me? Why?"

"Because you went out with Langfuss at night."

"He didn't tell me not to."

"In order not to insult Langfuss, he says."

"I don't understand anything."

"I understand only too well," whispered Batsheva. "He's got everything planned down to the last detail."

Riva did not reply, but she examined Batsheva's eyes for a moment to assess the extent of her lucidity. Her eyes were wet, but the expression in them together with her words showed that she was in full possession of her wits.

"You wouldn't understand, Riva, it's too complicated for your simple common sense."

"I believe in fate," said Riva mechanically. "There is a certain order in what seems to us accidental and inexplicable. Whatever we do, whatever others do, there is always a direction that is determined in advance."

"Langfuss has taught you something," said Batsheva.

Riva realized that she was talking wildly. "I don't know what I'm saying anymore. A person can go mad here. We need a house with a hundred rooms so that we can live together without ever seeing one another."

"Do me a favor, Riva, and stop talking about the new house, and about our houses in general. I'll be sick if I have to listen to another word on the subject. He plays with us and dangles bait before us, and like fools we run to swallow it. He's devilishly clever."

"Riva, come here for a moment," called Weiss from his room.

Riva looked at Batsheva in alarm, and the latter signaled her to go to her father.

"What's she telling you, your crazy sister?"

"Nothing, Father. We didn't talk about it."

"About what?"

"What do you want?"

"You have no understanding or character, Riva. You accept whatever she tells you, as if it were the truth. She's sick . . ."

"Sick?" laughed Batsheva, coming into the room. "And what did you say about her when she went out with Langfuss? What name did you call her?"

"Why did you suddenly decide to go to the colony, Riva?"

Riva stammered. Finally she said, "To get out of the house and get away from these arguments for a while. Why do you ask me? If you objected, a hint from you would have been enough for me to stay at home."

"I objected?" yelled Weiss furiously. "Me? I should object to your going out with Langfuss? I only wish something would come of it! I can't imagine a greater happiness for you, for me, for both of us."

Batsheva looked at Weiss in horror. "He's making fun of us, Riva," she said. "He's playing with us and changing his tune every five minutes to drive us out of our minds. Like he did to Mother. We're in his way, we're stopping him from doing something, I don't know what. He wants to get rid of us."

She marched out of the room.

Weiss grabbed hold of Riva's arm. "My little fool. I was glad when you went out with him but I was afraid, very afraid."

Riva did not understand. He turned his face in the direction of Batsheva's room. "I was afraid of her. She has no feeling, no family affection, not even for her sister. She said terrible things about you that I can't repeat. She compared you to Masha, who goes out to look for men at night. She said that you . . . you know what."

Riva said to herself, "I must hang on . . . hang on to the end and not go mad. I won't take any notice. I won't listen. I won't answer. I won't break down. I won't break down."

Weiss took up the Book of Psalms. A strange fever was burning in his eyes. His little gray beard gave him an alarmingly ascetic air. He said that he would not go to sleep and that he would say psalms all night for Batsheva's recovery and for peace in the family. All night long the light shone in Weiss's room, and his voice sawed through the air and kept them awake.

Batsheva grumbled from her bed, "As soon as he began to get religious I was suspicious. Now he's already lying awake all night muttering invocations from his holy book."

Riva could not understand her father's intentions. His muttering touched her heart. She stopped wondering about his satanic aims, his strange games with her and her sister, her own sanity. She asked herself what Langfuss would say if he knew, if he understood. His memory filled her with dejection, humiliation, and hatred.

Batsheva whispered from her bed, "Perhaps he doesn't feel well. He sounds delirious."

She got up and went to her father's bed in the next room and Riva heard her saying to him, "Father, do you feel all right? We've forgotten everything you said. I know you meant no harm. We forgive you and we love you. You must rest."

Batsheva pulled the sheet and the thin blanket up to his shoulders, tucked them round his little body, switched off the light, and said goodnight. He did not resist or say a single word. He only looked at her with fearful, imploring eyes, as if he were begging for his life.

A few hours later the dawn began to break.

Part Two:

FOUNDERS STREET

· 18 ·

BARUCH'S AGONY ENDURED FOR OVER A YEAR. GRADUALLY HE recovered his strength, but his fears did not diminish. He went back to work in the orange grove. His sleep was still troubled, but nevertheless he got up in the morning strong and refreshed, saddled his donkey, and rode to the grove. The recovery of his physical strength raised his spirits a little. He began to dream again of the girl he would bring one day as a gift to his aged mother, the girl he would carry into the house he had built for her with his own hands, but he didn't know how he would approach this girl and tell her of his heart's desire.

His donkey was clean and well groomed. He would stroke its belly and its wet face. He never whipped it or dug his heels into it. The donkey knew the road well and he trod it at a calm, leisurely pace. The mornings belonged to Baruch. There was hardly a soul stirring in the streets and he felt free, master of his fate and of the empty dew-drenched roads, the fragrant air. He would pass the small synagogue which stood not far from his house; there were always a few Jews scuttling about there and looking for a tenth man to make up the *minyan* for the morning prayers. Baruch hated all that.

Weiss was going to move into his new house that afternoon and Baruch had promised to help him. He knew that when Weiss saw his strong arms loading and then unloading their things, he would not think of firing him any more. Weiss's concern for his health, his demonstrations of affection, his praises, seemed to Baruch like a smoothing of the way for his eventual dismissal. He was still afraid of being fired.

On his way to the grove he passed the house in Train Street and saw Masha and her large family taking their bundles inside. He averted his face so that Masha would not see him. He hated her and felt ashamed in her presence. His ears caught the sound of her rude laughter, her shouts at her brother, little Napoleon, and he hurried his donkey forward. His heart wept for the trees he had planted for nothing, for his hoeing and weeding, fertilizing and watering. If he hadn't been too frightened and ashamed, he would have gone in the middle of the night and chopped them all down.

His hopes of recovery gave rise to great new plans in his heart. Weiss had told him about the orchard in the back yard of the house in Founders Street, and Baruch thought of cultivating it and making it famous throughout the colony and even throughout the entire district.

But in his dreams at night he sometimes found himself laying his hands on Mr. Weiss's money and raising his eyes to see the latter standing and looking at him. Baruch wanted to say something but his big hands muzzled his mouth. The money rolled over the floor clinking at his feet, evidence of his crime. Then all he wanted was to die—right away. At the sound of his groans his mother would rush into his room and find him bathed in sweat and sobbing, "I didn't mean to take anything."

She would wipe the sweat from his face with her warm sleeve, and he would hold the sleeve against his nose to smell his mother's smell, the beloved smell that made him feel peaceful and secure. There were nights when this dream recurred a number of times, and Baruch would get up in the morning wondering what it meant. For he had never in his life coveted a single penny that belonged to Mr. Weiss.

In any case Baruch did not enjoy even his own money. He gave it all to his mother, and she would say that she was saving it for his wedding. He had never even checked to see if the money was still there. He hated money.

He hoped that soon he would be rid of his sufferings at night too. He had not had his hair cut for a long time, and it grew all over his head and neck. A tangle of yellow flax. He hated his hair and he hated combing it.

When he entered the grove he saw the Arab workers and he thought that they were looking at him in a strange, embarrassed way. Perhaps they had heard from Weiss or from someone else of his dismissal?

He tried to smile at the workers and he spoke to them in their language, friendly as usual, but they answered him shortly, avoiding him and turning their backs on him. Now everything was quite clear to him. He wondered if Mirkin the miser would agree to have him back in his grove. He would explain to him that he didn't expect any special status, even though he had been an overseer for Mr. Weiss, and he would prove to him that he was still as strong as ever. He wouldn't say anything to his mother, in order not to upset her.

All day Baruch worked without joy. His sorrow gnawed at him, despite the consolations with which he tried to comfort himself. In the evening he left the grove without going to Mr. Weiss to help him, to spare him the embarrassment of telling him that he was fired.

He saddled his donkey, looked at the grove in which he

had worked as an overseer (he did not remember for how long), mounted the donkey, and ambled slowly down the dirt road. He passed old Mr. Levin's groves. The Arab guard recognized him and greeted him. It occurred to him to go to Mirkin's grove right away.

He continued along the dirt track after the turning that led to the colony. His donkey kept veering to the right as usual, and Baruch was obliged to kick him to make him turn left. He passed the gate of Mirkin's grove, but the guard told him there was nobody there. He looked right and the memory of the field hidden among the orange groves pierced him. His heart pounded and despite himself he turned the donkey onto the path.

Black and brown goats were grazing among the thorns, and with them a few cows. A little Arab girl was walking among them with a stick in her hand, goading them and gathering them together. The girl was the same girl! The moment was the same moment! And he thought that he had killed her. He pinched his legs to make sure that it wasn't one of his recurring nightmares. The little girl turned hither and thither and suddenly she saw his face and she uttered a loud scream. Two men, an old man and a boy, stood up behind the bushes at the end of the field and one of them asked, "Is that him?"

"That's him," cried the little girl, trembling in all her limbs.

Baruch turned to stone with dread. Only his shirt shook over his heart. His hands perspired. The donkey stood still and nibbled the thorns. Black and white spots danced before his eyes. His ears buzzed with cries and shouts, like the roar of an approaching train.

Two stabs in the ribs and the back, and his face smacked into the thorny ground. A terrible cold flooded his body. His nose bled. His father was dead and his mother screamed and rent her clothes. The black spots turned gray, merging with the white. Gray goats and white cows and rags stained with blood and dung.

WHILE HIS BODY was still warm the two men drew the knives from his flesh, undressed him, and did to him what he had done to the little girl.

Baruch's donkey looked at him with his moist, dumb eyes, lingered for a moment at his head, and did not recognize him. Baruch was naked. The men dragged him to the bottom of the field and flung his body far from the road. The donkey walked along the edge of the orange grove, reached the place where the road branched, and turned onto the road leading to the colony.

Nechama's neighbors sat on the bench and saw Baruch's donkey coming down the road. Nechama turned pale and felt the donkey's back and belly as if she were looking to see if Baruch was hiding inside him.

She hurried immediately to Train Street, her heart full of dread. On the way she asked people if they had seen Baruch. When she reached the house on Train Street, she saw Mr. Weiss and his daughters loading their belongings onto a cart and Masha's family wandering around the yard. She knew nothing about the new house and she thought that all the commotion was somehow connected with Baruch.

Weiss went out with Nechama to the grove. The people they passed on the road did not know Baruch. Levin's guard had seen Baruch turn left, which he did not usually do. Mirkin's guard had spoken to Baruch. Baruch had asked him if Mirkin was in the grove. He had said that he was interested in working for him. Weiss understood nothing. What did Baruch want with Mirkin?

They went into the field. The field was empty, but the smell of the goats and the dung still rose from it like hot steam. Weiss did not see anything, but Nechama ran in terror to the end of the field. Next to the bushes Baruch lay naked.

For a moment Weiss lost consciousness. Then he saw Nechama covering Baruch's nakedness with her body. She said nothing. She did not weep, she did not scream.

After dark the police came. They dragged Nechama off Baruch's body. She said weakly, "You should be ashamed of yourselves. Can't you see, he's naked."

When she came home she sat down on the bench. Not a single one of her neighbors came to sit down beside her, to take care of her needs. Nechama cursed her neighbors. Late that night she went into the house and closed the windows and the doors. When she went up to Baruch's bed she saw his old slippers at the foot of the bed, his pillow and his blankets peeping from under the bedspread. She beat her hands together, ran to the window next to his bed, and cried, "Thieves, robbers, murderers! Thieves! Robbers! Murderers!"

She stood and screamed all night long, and all the following nights, until the neighbors got used to it and it no longer kept them awake. Her bench remained deserted and forlorn. A stranger who came upon the place by chance and sat down on the bench to rest would jump up and run at the sound of Nechama's voice rising from the house.

· 19 ·

WHEN HE CAME HOME FROM THE FUNERAL WEISS WALKED AROUND his orange grove, and it seemed to him that it had lost all its meaning. From now on it was simply a collection of trees from which he earned his living and no more. He was tormented by the thought of all kinds of injustices he imagined he had done Baruch during the time he had worked for him. He had no idea where he would get a new overseer or how he would be able to trust him. He himself could not supervise the work. He was afraid of degenerating like the other farmers and turning into an Arab like them. The memory of Baruch's strong body, his flaxen hair, his little eyes, the eyes of an aged child, the dancing hoe in his clumsy hands, broke his heart in two.

Apathetically he settled down in his new house, in the place his daughters allocated to him. At first the three of them moved about the house like strangers. The large rooms, the long corridors, the big orchard at the back, were full of mysteries and terrors. The smell of the house too was strange and repellent. Weiss was given a room with a window overlooking the garden and the fence separating them from the neighbor's house. Riva and Batsheva each took one of the inner rooms overlooking the orchard because the front rooms were too big for them.

For a long time they were even afraid to touch the strange furniture and the tasseled curtains. The memory of the little pale woman still weighed heavily on the house. And even though they were now living in the heart of the colony, surrounded by many houses, they felt less secure here than they had felt on Train Street.

During the first weeks all Weiss wanted to do was rest. He had not yet found a new overseer, and he did hardly anything to find one. He waited for someone to come and offer him his services.

The plumber pulled down half the kitchen wall and installed an additional sink. Weiss examined all the *mezzuzas* on the doorposts to make sure that they were as they should be, and added new ones where they were lacking. He spent his evenings in the big synagogue. He and Shor the Monk avoided any mention of the unfortunate Sabbath meal. They felt friendship for each other, but Weiss no longer invited him to dine at his house.

After the holidays the picking season began. The need for a new overseer became urgent. Langfuss was not forthcoming and said that he had no suitable candidate for the job. In the end it occurred to Weiss to offer the job to Masha's father. The appearance of the pale, unemployed man did nothing to inspire his confidence, but the fact that he would be able to deduct the rent from his wages was an advantage.

When he entered the old house in Train Street, he was greeted by Masha's mother, her face shining as usual with respectful gratitude and meekness. Masha's father was lying in bed in his pajamas, pale and unshaven. Mrs. Hershkovitz chased the children out of the room and her husband sat up in bed.

"I've come to you with a very important proposition, Mr. Hershkovitz," said Weiss with affected solemnity.

"Leave the room," said the pale man to Masha's mother, "and go to the kitchen."

Masha's mother immediately left the room.

"What is this proposition?" asked Hershkovitz.

"Do you know anything about work in a citrus grove?" asked Weiss.

"Why do you ask, Mr. Weiss?"

"I know that you're out of work and I want to help you."

"You want me to work for you?"

"Yes," said Weiss, and when he saw the man looking at him without responding he added, "As overseer."

"Dvora!" cried Masha's father loudly.

His wife hurried into the room and stood beside him waiting expectantly.

"I'm unemployed," said Mr. Hershkovitz. "I've never worked in the citrus groves. I've always been unemployed."

"He's a sick man," explained his wife. "He's not allowed to work."

Her husband confirmed her words with a nod of his head.

"But he doesn't have to work," said Weiss. "Only to see that the Arabs work and present me with the accounts."

He looked at them in despair.

"And if they kill me, your Arabs, like they killed Baruch?" asked Mr. Hershkovitz.

Weiss had no satisfactory answer to this. The very mention of Baruch's name by this man revolted him.

"You know that the police found the murderers today?" said Hershkovitz.

"They found them?" cried Weiss.

"Certainly," said Mr. Hershkovitz calmly. "Workers from your grove. They told them why they killed Baruch too and why they did that terrible thing to him. Dvora, leave the room and shut the door behind you."

Masha's mother left the room and shut the door behind her.

"Don't you know anything?" asked Hershkovitz.

"No," said Weiss, waiting to hear something terrible.

"He raped a little Arab shepherdess. Her family found him, killed him, and raped him like he did to her."

"And everybody in the colony knows about it?"

"Of course," he said. "And if they don't know yet, they will soon."

Weiss stood up, said a weak goodbye, and went home. In the salon he found a dark young man with a thin face and a long nose, who refused to tell Weiss who had sent him. He offered his services as overseer in Weiss's grove. He was new to the colony; he had come from the Galilee a few days before.

The next day Weiss took him to the orange grove. His name was Ben-Zioni. Yechiel Ben-Zioni, and he was familiar with the work. But he didn't lift a finger himself, all he did was wander to and fro talking to the Arabs. Weiss asked him if he wasn't afraid. The man laughed and shrugged his shoulders. He wasn't in the least like Baruch. But the picking season was upon them and Weiss had no choice.

Ben-Zioni had little to say to Weiss, but Weiss thought him reliable. He offered him a room in his house, but the new overseer refused politely. Weiss tried to persuade him, even offering him the room for nothing. Ben-Zioni smiled and said that he preferred to live alone. Weiss regarded this reply as insulting and insolent, but he said nothing.

The picking was concluded without any problems and the yield was good. Hadassah gave birth to a baby girl and she called her Esther, after her mother. The teacher Borochov did not leave the baby's side all spring. Hadassah bloomed after the birth, her face resumed its former delicacy and her eyes their sad glow.

In moments of emotion the teacher Borochov thought of writing down the poem that he had borne in his heart for so many years. In his imagination he could see the main lines and hear the rhythm of the poem. When summer came he despaired and his spirits fell again.

ONCE THE WEISSES had grown accustomed to the new house, their confidence returned and they began to spend their nights in the usual quarrels and recriminations. Weiss began to speak of going up to Jerusalem, to pray at the Western Wall.

"It's deadly dangerous now," said Riva.

Batsheva thought that he was trying to frighten them and make them feel sorry for him. But after he had spent the whole winter talking about it, he got up one day in the spring and went up to Jerusalem. He intended staying there for a week. When he parted from his daughters, he kissed them like someone setting out on a long journey and mentioned casually that just to be on the safe side, he had already made his will and they had nothing to worry about. Riva felt that she would not see her father alive again. Ever since Baruch's death Weiss had claimed that in the end the Arabs would murder him too. His talk of a will brought a chill into Batsheva's gray eyes and sent a spasm through her cheeks. The first night after Weiss's departure for Jerusalem Riva could not sleep. She pulled the blanket over her head so that Batsheva sleeping in the next room would not hear her cry. This journey of her father's, which Batsheva regarded as one more sign of his insanity, seemed to Riva like an act of martyrdom, deliberate and inevitable. The fear that gnawed at her was not a fear for his safety but an obscure dread that she could not comprehend, a dread that convulsed her body and cut off her breath.

The next morning she wandered by herself through the rooms of the big house as if she had lost her way or was searching for something. When Batsheva came home Riva fawned on her as if she was all she had left in the world. After a few days Weiss's absence no longer weighed on the house. The nights were long and peaceful, the old novels were unpacked from the parcel in which they had been moved from the old house, and Batsheva said that on summer evenings they would sit in the front garden with its tall shady trees, soft green lawn, and high concrete wall hiding the house from the street.

A week after his departure Weiss had not yet come home. After two days of worry they received a letter in which he reassured them and informed them that he would be coming home, God willing, in a week's time.

Her father's letter affected Riva strongly, but she was ashamed to reveal her emotion to Batsheva and pretended to be as indifferent as she was.

A week later Weiss came home bringing an old woman with him. The old woman was Chasida, Friedman the drunk's sister-in-law. He had married her during his stay in Jerusalem, and on his return he treated her like a young bridegroom. He showered her with affectionate pet names and compliments, and for the first time since Baruch's death he laughed in wholehearted enjoyment of his new wife's witticisms. Whenever she opened her mouth to speak in the dialect peculiar to those born in Jerusalem, he broke into a smile. He appeared to love her very much.

The old woman smiled at the flabbergasted girls with affection and sympathy.

"The season of love is upon us," muttered Batsheva in horror.

· 20 ·

CHASIDA WAS HADASSAH FRIEDMAN'S MOTHER'S SISTER. SHE was older than Weiss, and his daughters decided to call her "Grandma." She was a lean woman with a thin, bony face and she wore a brown wig, the same color as her deep eyes. She had been living alone for many years as a widow in Jerusalem, in a small room not far from the Hurva Synagogue. That, at any rate, was what she said, for no one had ever been to her home in Jerusalem.

Despite her age, Chasida was a vigorous, hardworking woman. She immediately adapted herself to the routine of her new home, took over all the work, and refused to employ a maid. Riva was left with nothing to do. Her father suggested that she go back to work as a seamstress, but when he saw that his daughter was unenthusiastic about his proposal, he left her alone. The house was clean and sparkling as never before. Weiss embraced the old woman, kissing her wig, and

Chasida said, "Pfui, you ought to be ashamed, an old man like you, and a pious Jew too."

"AT LEAST I CAN be sure that what I eat is absolutely kosher," Weiss said to his daughters. "Who knows what you two put in the dishes you cooked for me, a pair of brazen atheists like you."

The first week after the new Mrs. Weiss's arrival in the colony, Weiss asked her to join him in a visit to her brother-in-law, Friedman, her niece Hadassah and Hadassah's new baby girl.

Chasida raised her eyebrows. "Me go to visit that drunk? Let him come visit me here, in my home, if his legs can still carry him so far."

When the news reached Friedman and he was persuaded that it was really true that his sister-in-law had married Weiss and that she was living in his house, he came one evening with Hadassah to visit her. The teacher Borochov stayed at home with the baby.

"I'm not drunk, Chasida, I'm not drunk now," Friedman announced the moment he came in the door.

"With you it's impossible to tell," said Chasida.

"Oh Chasida, Chasida," replied Friedman, "married or not married, you haven't changed."

"Neither have you, Friedman," said Chasida. "You won't change until the day you die like a drunken dog in the street."

"Pfui, Chasida, what kind of a way is that to talk? You'll have to forget the language you used with your friends in the markets of Jerusalem. Now you're part of an important, respectable family. Mr. Weiss isn't a fishmonger or a shoe-maker or a cartdriver like me."

Weiss invited them to come inside, not stand there in the doorway. In the living room Chasida embraced Hadassah and would not let her go. Hadassah blushed in embarrassment at the old woman's insistent affection.

"I'm so glad, Aunt Chasida, that you're here with us. In the colony they say there's rioting in Jerusalem now."

"It's dangerous everywhere and it's safe everywhere," Chasida said. "Everything depends on the individual and on God."

"When you're together with your family in the same place, you feel better," said Hadassah.

"That's something else," said the old woman firmly.

"She's getting younger, this woman," sniggered Friedman.

Weiss asked the girls to serve refreshments to their guests. They got up unwillingly and went to the kitchen.

"How about a little drink, Friedman?" asked Weiss.

"What else?" said Friedman. "On an occasion like this? When you get married for the second time round I realize you don't throw a big party for the whole world. But a little drink is a *mitzva*! For good luck. *Mazeltov* and may all the Jews be happy and all the Arabs die!"

The drinks had not yet arrived when he concluded his speech and he looked about in regret for the words he had spoken in vain. Weiss stood up and poured a small glass of brandy for himself and for Friedman and a drop for Chasida too. The girls brought cookies, oranges left over from the winter, and candies.

Friedman said, "*Mazeltov*, good luck, and may all the Jews . . ."

"You've said that already," interrupted Chasida. "There's no need to repeat exactly the same thing twice. He who was supposed to hear has already heard."

"You haven't seen our baby yet," said Hadassah.

"I haven't seen Borochov yet either."

"He stayed home with the baby. We named her after my mother, may she rest in peace, Esther."

"Oy . . ." sighed Chasida, and said no more.

Riva and Batsheva joined them at the table after they had served the refreshments.

"And how are the girls, Weiss?" asked Friedman.

They smiled sweetly and tilted their heads archly.

"When are you going to make up your minds to get married?" asked Friedman when the brandy began to go to his head. "If you wait too long, you'll wait forever."

Weiss blushed and said, "Everything will be all right, Friedman, don't worry."

"What do you mean, all right? My Hadassah is younger than they are and she already has a baby, whom she's named after my late wife, may she rest in peace. If we don't have children, who will we name after our departed loved ones, and who will be named for us when we've gone to heaven?"

"And who told you, Friedman, that you're going straight to heaven?" asked Chasida.

"Chasida and her wisecracks," Friedman winked at the others and flapped his hand at her in a gesture of dismissal and despair. "If it was up to her to decide who went to heaven and hell, she would sit in Paradise devouring the wild ox and the Leviathan of the righteous all by herself."

Weiss smiled with enjoyment at this exchange between his wife and her brother-in-law, but after a glance at the bored faces of his daughters sitting at the end of the table, he seemed to wake from a sweet dream and his brow darkened.

He realized that his laughter was out of place and that it pierced his daughters like poisoned arrows. Friedman gobbled the cookies and Hadassah poked him with her elbow to make him stop.

"Stop it, Hadassah, we're among family here," protested Friedman. "Aren't we?" he asked.

"Of course," replied Batsheva, and her voice sent shivers down Chasida's spine.

Friedman looked pitifully at his empty glass and winked at Weiss. Weiss pretended not to notice the hint. Chasida moved her chair closer to Hadassah and asked her in a whisper about her father's condition and behavior.

Friedman overheard and said, "I haven't changed, Chasida. You said so yourself. I still drink a lot in order to enjoy whatever life is left to me. And where have you found it written that it's forbidden to drink?"

"And you comply with everything that *is* written, do you?" said Chasida.

"Look at her," giggled Friedman, "answering a question with another question."

"How would you like me to answer you?" said Chasida. "With a dance?"

Hadassah got up to go.

Friedman said, "What's this, Hadassah? Let me stay a little with my sister-in-law. I haven't seen her for such a long time, not since . . ."

"Since the wedding," Chasida reminded him. "I remember only too well."

"Really? So you remember it, do you?" retorted Friedman sarcastically.

"Yes," she replied. "We all remember the father of the bride, his perfect manners, his courtly behavior."

"Anyone would think you were born in a royal palace."

Chasida did not reply. Hadassah helped her father up and they parted from their hosts after the latter had promised to return the visit and come to see the new baby and the teacher Borochov. When they had gone there was a short silence, which Batsheva broke by saying, "Our family has come up in the world."

"What's wrong, Batsheva? Are you afraid they'll spoil your chances of getting a husband? I haven't seen the brilliant matches that have come your way because of our family connections up to now. I haven't seen the suitors lining up at the door to ask for your hand or for your sister's."

Chasida said in dismay, "Haim, what are you talking about? Are you paying attention to that drunk? The girls are still young and there's no need to keep nagging them about husbands and matches. When the time comes, you'll know."

"Chasida," sighed Weiss. "You don't know anything. You'll find out soon enough."

Chasida smiled encouragingly at the girls, but they plainly needed no encouragement. She stood up and began clearing the dishes and taking them to the kitchen, where she started washing up. Weiss left the girls in the living room and joined her in the kitchen.

"What sink are you using now?" asked Weiss.

"The milk sink. But there's no difference. I don't leave the dishes in the sink, and these dishes are neither milk nor meat."

"Good," said Weiss, pleased that she had passed the test.

"It's better to know everything in advance," said Chasida, "to be ready for the blow when it comes."

"You have an answer ready for everything, Chasida. Where does a woman get so much sense from?"

"You chatter like a child," said Chasida, and her shoulders shook.

"How can the blow be avoided, when you yourself always say, 'Man thinks and God laughs.' "

"What do you suggest, that people should stop thinking? Thinking is a *mitzva* too."

"Two old people like us," said Weiss joyfully, "coming together at our age, and happy as a pair of teenagers."

Chasida said nothing but Weiss saw the smile breaking through the wrinkles around her mouth as she bent over the sink.

Weiss's eyes misted over. He wanted to make her happy

and he didn't know what to do for her. Perhaps he should pick her up and carry her to her room and tell her what was in his heart—what things had been like before and what they were like now. Perhaps he should touch her plain, spotlessly clean clothes, so aristocratic in their modesty, and smell their fragrance and kiss them. She would laugh at him and smile with her deep brown eyes. With the corners of her mouth, with her thin lips, she would tease him like a mother teases a naughty child. And that he did not want.

Riva was lying in bed and reading when Batsheva came in and sat down. She put her book down and looked at her sister, full of foreboding.

"Everything's happening just as I predicted," said Batsheva. "And I can already see the end."

"Didn't you know why he was going to Jerusalem?" asked Riva.

"I knew he was going to do something crazy. A man of his age. It's a disgrace."

"He's not so old."

"He's carrying on like a lovesick boy."

"He needs it," said Riva.

"It isn't normal, Riva. He's losing his mind. I saw it developing gradually. It began with trivial little things and it's ending in this calamity."

"But they don't even sleep in the same room," said Riva.

"You're a baby, Riva, you don't know the first thing about life."

"I've read the same novels you have."

"But I've learned a lot more from them than you have."

"She doesn't bother me so much."

"You're too submissive. All you're ever wanted is to please other people. An inferiority complex, that's what you've got. When that drunk sat there in our living room, I saw it as a symbol of our situation."

"Our situation was never fantastic."

"But at least we were proud and kept ourselves to ourselves."

"In order to hide all the quarrels and the madness."

"You're in a strange mood, Riva. You look as if you're going to your death with an easy mind. You look as if you've fallen in love."

"You're full of ideas today."

"Tell the truth, Riva, you know you can't hide anything from me."

"I don't know what you want of me."

"There's a lot you don't know about me, Riva, and that you couldn't imagine either, and if you did know you would be frightened out of your wits and your hair would stand on end."

"You're not scaring me."

"When you and father went to Langfuss one Saturday night to close the deal about the new house, Borochov suddenly turned up. He must have known I was home alone. I can't bring myself to tell you what he said and did."

"Did he make love to you?"

"Yes."

"All the way?"

"Yes."

Riva was horrified. She had never heard anything like this from her sister before. There was a smile in Batsheva's blue eyes that Riva could only call wanton. Now she believed it all, and a shudder of revulsion convulsed her body and pounded in her temples.

"You're mad, Batsheva. Whether what you say is true or not, this is the talk of a crazy woman."

"You may be right," sighed Batsheva, and she smiled patronizingly at her sister.

"What now?" asked Riva.

"Now goodnight," said Batsheva, getting up from Riva's bed. She opened the door and apologized to her father, who was trying to eavesdrop, for banging it into his forehead. He blustered, "What are you two whispering about all night long, keeping the whole house awake?" Without troubling to reply Batsheva retired to her room and shut the door behind her.

· 21 ·

CHASIDA'S CLOTHES WERE ALWAYS CLEAN AND NEAT, HER SHOES always polished, her eyes always smiling. She was the first to rise, early in the morning, to prepare breakfast for Weiss and Batsheva. Riva would get up late, for there was nothing left for her to do in the house. When the *hamsin* season came, Chasida began to suffer. It was very hot, but she did not complain and the smile never left her eyes. She would tell them about Jerusalem, the fresh days and cool nights, the paved streets, the markets next to the Western Wall, and the Hurva Synagogue near her house.

"What can you know about Jerusalem if you've never been there?" she would say with a dreamy smile.

"Are you homesick?" asked Weiss.

"One always longs for what is far away, especially for Jerusalem," replied Chasida. "It is the Holy City, after all."

Weiss would grow gloomy when she began telling her stories about Jerusalem. The Jerusalem he had seen was nothing but a pile of stones, filthy Arab bazaars, crowds and commotion and ruins. For fear of sinning with his lips, he did not dare voice these criticisms aloud.

"The air of Jerusalem," said Chasida, "has a holy sweetness about it, a real tonic."

She looked at them sadly, as if she suspected that her stories did not interest them.

"And on the Sabbath everyone who owns a house paints the walls blue inside and out, every week, and the stone floors shine, and nobody goes inside with their outdoor shoes on, so as not to dirty the floors. Already on Thursday the smell of the Sabbath dishes rises from the outside ovens in the courtyards; the smell of the Sabbath bread baking and the houses spread a smell of cleanliness throughout the town, a smell of freshly painted walls. And the Sabbath in Jerusalem, with the sound of the prayers in the Hurva reaching right to my window—ah, the angels of heaven are there . . ."

She fell silent and her eyes were wet, smiled shamefacedly at her own weakness, and went out to water the lawn in order to freshen the air in the garden. She would stand watering the garden for hours to bring back the coolness that had been lost to her in her new home.

On Fridays Chasida would drag herself all the way to the big market, in the heat of the summer, to buy provisions cheap. Weiss tried to stop her, explaining that they were not poor people and it shamed him for his wife to run to the other end of the colony to save a few pennies. She said, "The prices here are outrageous," and took no notice of his pleas. She was a stubborn woman, and she always found an excuse for everything she did. She would come home laden with heavy baskets, panting and perspiring, and nobody would help her to unpack her load.

Her room was one of the largest in the house, with black furniture. Both its windows overlooked the orchard. In one corner stood her bed with the mattress and green silk bedspread she had brought with her from Jerusalem. On one of the bureaus she placed a few photographs and a few shabby black handbags from which she refused to part. All day the room was dim and cool in the shade of the orchard trees sheltering her windows.

Weiss found her cooking to his taste, but Batsheva complained that the food was still pervaded by the smell of the dung in the outdoor ovens of Jerusalem. Chasida did not understand what dung had to do with outdoor ovens, or what outdoor ovens had to do with her cooking, or perhaps she pretended not to understand for the sake of peace and quiet. Although Weiss asked her not to take any notice of what the girls, especially Batsheva, said, Chasida was afraid that the blow that Weiss had hinted at might find her unprepared and unable to defend herself. The stares and strange ways and looks of Weiss's daughters began to terrify her, and since she did not know exactly what they meant, the fear was obscure and thus even harder to bear. One day she discovered that her belongings on the bureau were not set out as usual, as if someone had been rummaging among them. After a while she noticed the disorder again, and this time she realized that it was not a coincidence or absent-mindedness on her part.

The fact that the girls hardly spoke to her and gave her hostile and contemptuous looks she had interpreted at first as jealousy for the dead mother's sake, but the way they whispered together or with their father, behind her back or in her presence, the interference with her belongings in her room, and the arguments they conducted with their father in mysterious hints alerted her to be on her guard. But she did not know how to guard herself or from which direction the blow would come. Of one thing she was sure: Whatever happened, even if she was at the end of her tether, she would not tell anyone or beg for charity from the Friedmans. No one would know of her suffering and shame.

The streets of the Old City of Jerusalem now seemed to her like scenes from a remote childhood, and she no longer knew what was true in these scenes and what she herself had added to her homesickness. The faces of the friends she had left behind were already fading from her mind, and each of them had been reduced to one single feature, prominent and characteristic, which she remembered. One had a mole on her chin, another a heavy body and a squeaky voice, another was a terrible gossip, and so on and so forth. Only the sound of the people praying in the Hurva still rang clearly in her ears at moments of grace. And these moments were rare. Most of them came at night and a few in the morning when there was nobody at home, not even Riva.

Riva was weak. Her obscure fear of her sister enslaved her to the latter's eccentricities. Chasida wondered if she would ever succeed in understanding these sisters and their peculiar ways. Haim Weiss advised her to ignore them for the sake of her peace of mind, but in the depths of his heart he suffered torments and he tried to hide his distress from her. When she decided to accept his proposal of marriage, Chasida had smiled to herself, almost like Sarah behind the tent in the Bible, in skepticism and shame. The change seemed too sudden and too fortunate to last. But in the end she believed in her good fortune and accepted it enthusiastically. "Man thinks and God laughs." Woe to that laughter!

Whenever she opened her mouth to say something, they would burst out laughing, as if they had just heard a hilarious joke. She would attempt to make some remark and the two of them would chorus, "Where I come from in Jerusalem . . ."

Haim Weiss would turn pale with anger but refrain from rebuking his daughters for fear that a quarrel would erupt. And when they saw that he did not react, they spoke more and more wildly, Batsheva laughing loudly and Riva aping her.

Chasida had never in her life felt such hatred directed against her. She herself had never hated anyone, not even the wretched Friedman. Even her landlords in Jerusalem, with whom she had lived for so many years for such a small rent, were kind and friendly to her, and ever since she had been widowed they would come to visit her every Sabbath, so that she would not be lonely and unhappy on the day of rest.

"What harm have I done them for them to hate me so much?" she asked Haim Weiss.

"It's only Batsheva," said Weiss. "Riva doesn't know what she's doing."

"Explain to them that I have no heirs and they need have no fears about their property."

"I've already made arrangements for you to remain in this house after my death as long as you live. After that the house will go to whichever of them marries first."

"You're forgetting that I'm older than you."

"Women live longer than men, Chasida, and I don't begrudge it you." After a silence he added, "But I don't envy anyone who will have to stay here with them alone."

"You say terrible things."

"You, for all your wisdom, can't possibly understand. You're too simple and too decent to understand what I'm saying."

Then she decided to tell him about the searches in her belongings on the bureau. Weiss was furious and he immediately summoned his daughters. They presented themselves with bored, tired expressions on their faces.

"What is the meaning of these searches in Chasida's room?" he yelled.

Batsheva raised her eyebrows. "I'm out at work all day, and when I come home Grandma is with me. You cannot suspect me of such things."

Weiss looked at the frightened and blushing Riva.

"Riva!" he yelled as he had never yelled at her before. Tears of insult came into Riva's eyes and she muttered to Batsheva, "We'll have to tell him everything."

"Of course you have to tell me everything," shouted Weiss, "and immediately!"

"I have no secrets in my room," said Chasida quietly, as if she was explaining something to a small child. "But if someone conducts a search it means he is looking for something. I would like to know what."

Riva wept and Batsheva said coldly, "Let her leave the room."

Chasida made haste to leave the room, but Weiss called her back immediately. "I have no secrets from her. She is *my wife*, do you understand? My wife!"

"Your wife is ill with a fatal disease," said Batsheva.

The blood drained from Chasida's face.

"*You're* ill! You're insane!" screamed Weiss. "What rubbish are you talking now?"

"She is ill with kleptomania," said Batsheva calmly, as if she had not been interrupted at all.

Chasida was on the point of collapse. The terrible word whose meaning she did not understand put the fear of death into her, and she almost believed that she had indeed succumbed to this mysterious disease.

"What's that?" asked Weiss.

"The stealing sickness," said Batsheva. "The need to steal, not for gain, but out of a psychological compulsion."

Chasida said imploringly, "Batsheva, why do you say such things about me? What harm have I ever done you?"

Batsheva did not even hear her. She fixed her clear blue eyes on her father and said, "It may not be pleasant, but it's the truth and it has to be told."

Chasida fell onto the chair and hung her head. Weiss stood up and patted her shoulders encouragingly. "Now you understand, Chasida, now you know everything. The girl is insane. This is her insanity speaking. She ought to be put away. You will have to try to put up with it and take no notice. For the sake of your health and peace of mind."

Chasida did not reply, but his words seemed to move her. The wrinkles on her face around her eyes filled with anxiety and her left eyelid began to quiver. But she didn't cry.

Riva explained, "That's why she insists on going to the big market. It's easier for her there. Nobody knows her, it's crowded and busy, and there's plenty of everything lying about, like in her Jerusalem."

"Rivaleh," begged Weiss, "you're letting your sister confuse you. You're not saying what you really think. You're a good girl, a decent girl. What's happening to you? What's happening to us? What are we coming to? What did we buy a house like this for, for it to be empty and dead, full of disappointment and madness?"

Chasida rose laboriously to her feet and went to the kitchen to wash the dishes. Weiss remained with his silent daughters.

"I don't know what I'm saying, Father," confessed Riva. "But I want to stay sane and lucid to the end."

Batsheva's whole body rose up in protest against this betrayal. "Sweet little Riva, Daddy and Grandma's darling."

"Hold your tongue, you madwoman."

"You know the truth, Father, don't you, so what's the point of yelling?"

"I would tell you to go and fall on your knees before that wonderful woman, kiss her feet and beg her pardon, if I didn't know that you were unworthy to stand beside her."

"You hear, Riva?" said Batsheva. "Doesn't it remind you of something? The way he used to talk about Shor the Monk?"

"Shut up! Do you hear? Shut up before they put you away!" screamed Weiss and his lips turned white.

Chasida stood by the sink and washed the dishes. Her hands shook and a big china plate slipped out of her fingers and broke. The pieces scattered all over the floor. Chasida stood there with her two wet hands stuck out in front of her as if she were paralyzed. The tears started to well out of the slits of her eyes and flow soundlessly between her wrinkles to her nose and chin. Her left eyelid quivered nervously and the corners of her mouth twitched.

At the sound of the plate breaking Weiss hurried to the kitchen. He embraced her head and said, "What is it, my Chasidaleh? Why are you crying? For a miserable broken plate, for something not worth a penny? It only grieves me when you cry. I have enough grief without it. A clever woman like you, crying for nonsense?"

Chasida bent down and picked up the pieces one by one.

"Perhaps it will bring us good luck, Chasida," said Weiss. "Good luck, Chasida, good luck!"

· 22 ·

IT WAS A VERY HOT SUMMER THAT YEAR, AND CHASIDA SUFFERED from the heat. Weiss forgot, or tried to make her forget, the subject of the "terrible disease," but Batsheva kept hinting at it and would not let the matter drop. She even claimed that she had definite proof of Chasida's kleptomania. Weiss refused to listen to her proofs, told her to get out of his sight, and said that she was insane. He was demonstratively loving to Chasida to annoy Batsheva, but she remained cool and composed and announced that he would not succeed in destroying her like he had destroyed her mother.

During all the time that Batsheva worked at the bank, she hardly noticed the people around her. She was polite and reserved. Nachum Shlomi worked in an office near hers, but she had never given him a thought. One day he paused at her desk to take a sheet of paper, and his warm breath brushed her neck. At that moment Batsheva felt as if a heavy burden had been lifted from her heart. After that there were moments of embarrassment and stolen smiles, warm greetings, distraction, and sleeplessness. No one at home knew anything about it.

Every day he would accompany her from the bank to Founders Street, and these moments kept Batsheva going all day long. Chasida thought that everything was back to normal again. The house was quiet. Batsheva stopped her nervous laughter, her hostile hints, and her eyes were dreamy. Weiss wanted to reconcile with her and get back her affection, but when Riva said to him, "Batsheva is calm, too calm. I can sense disaster in the air," he replied, "That's a bad sign. Very bad. The sickness is gaining control over her and she's going quietly insane." When he saw that Riva was alarmed, he said, "Please God, let us all be healthy."

Nachum Shlomi invited Batsheva to go with him to a cafe in Tel Aviv after work. They sat in the twilight at a little round table in a boulevard cafe. Nachum Shlomi was embarrassed at first and Batsheva felt that he wanted to say something to her about his love. When they left the cafe it was already completely dark. He embraced her, and they sauntered slowly arm in arm to the end of the boulevard until they reached the shore, and then they turned and walked back up the boulevard again.

Batsheva's first night of love ended next to the water tower, on the hill next to her house. He accompanied her to the gate, where they lingered for a long time, unable to part.

The front door had been left open. It was late, Batsheva did not know how late. She imagined that they must have been worried about her, perhaps they had even gone to look for her, but she didn't care.

He was the most beautiful man she had ever seen. Not the kind of beauty that conquers the heart immediately, but the kind that penetrates it gradually, refined and noble, worthy of her love. Shlomi was dark, his face as sharply defined as the face of an ancient statue. His body full but not fat, a little taller than she was with small delicate ears and a long, slender neck. His Adam's apple stuck out and quivered when he was embarrassed. He knew how to treat her; he spoke calmly and rather loudly, but there was an agreeable huskiness in his voice. When he whispered into her ear, a tremor of warmth and delight rose in her breast and spread through all her body as she breathed.

All night long she lay burning on her bed, and the following morning nobody said anything about her absence. The next day and the next they made love on the sands of Tel Aviv and among the orange groves of the colony. That whole week Batsheva came home late, when everyone was already in bed. But Weiss and Riva heard her coming in barefoot every night and tiptoeing to her room.

Weiss said to Riva, "I'm afraid. She's likely to poison herself on one of these walks and bring a catastrophe down on herself and the whole family."

Riva guessed what was going on and she seethed with fury and outrage.

After a week of sleepless nights Weiss made Batsheva sit down opposite him and explain. Riva stood to one side, waiting anxiously to hear what Batsheva would say.

"You know, Father, so why ask?" said Batsheva.

"I know nothing," said Weiss.

"I'm going out with someone."

Weiss jumped up, pale and dismayed.

"I love somebody and he loves me."

"Riva!" Weiss appealed for pity. "The girl is insane. I've been saying so for years and no one pays any attention to me."

"Why is she insane?" Chasida intervened. "I don't understand what insanity has to do with it. The girl is in love with a boy. She'll marry him. What's wrong with that?"

Weiss said nothing. He covered his eyes with his hand and groaned.

"You won't stop me whatever you do," whispered Bat-sheva.

"Who is the man?" asked Weiss.

"What do you want to know his name for?" said Batsheva in alarm.

"My daughter is going out every night with a young man and I'm not allowed to know his name?"

"His name is Shlomi."

"Shlomi what?"

"Nachum Shlomi."

"What's his first name and what's his family name?"

"Nachum is his first name and Shlomi is his family name."

"Has he got a family at all?"

"Yes."

"Where did you meet him?"

"At the bank," smiled Batsheva.

"Is he from the colony?" asked Weiss.

"Yes."

Weiss asked no more questions and he seemed reassured. Batsheva breathed a sign of relief. When she left the room Riva went out with her and whispered, "Whore!"

Batsheva smiled a superior smile and said nothing. She walked proudly to her room, took her bag, said goodbye, and went to work.

Just before lunchtime Weiss went to the bank. He stood nearby and waited for the employees to come out for their lunch break. Finally he saw Batsheva arm in arm with a young man. He stood in his hiding place and waited until they were out of sight. The next day he went back and observed the young man again. The day after that he saw Batsheva coming out of the bank alone and concluded that her boyfriend had remained inside. As soon as she was a little way off he went quickly into the bank.

One of the employees told him that they were closed for lunch. Weiss replied that he only wanted to find out if there was a clerk in the bank by the name of Nachum Shlomi. The man replied in the affirmative and Weiss asked to see him.

"Just a moment," said the clerk curtly, and went into the next room. The door opened and the young man emerged. Weiss went up to him.

"Are you Nachum Shlomi?" he asked.

"Yes, sir," said the boy. "And who are you?"

"I am Batsheva's father, Haim Weiss."

Shlomi smiled shyly and put out his hand, but Weiss rejected it, glared at him with eyes full of hate, and suddenly spat with all his strength, cursed him, and walked away.

When he came home he found them all sitting around the table and waiting for him, Chasida full of concern as he had never before been late for a meal. Without a word he sat down and began to eat. As soon as he had taken the edge off his hunger, he smiled complacently and began to joke. Chasida thought that everything had taken a turn for the better. Batsheva retired to her room to rest until the lunch break was over, and Riva went on sitting at the table reading a book. Chasida cleared the dishes off the table and went into the kitchen.

"Everything will be all right, Riva," said Weiss with a happy smile.

Riva said nothing. She nodded her head and went on reading. Weiss despaired of her and went out to the orchard. The crop had not been particularly good that winter but he was not concerned. From the day Baruch died he had lost interest in his orange grove.

Batsheva went back to work. Riva lay down to rest and Chasida set to work to clean the house. Weiss sat in the living room in the big armchair, trying unsuccessfully to doze. It was very hot and the walls of the house were beginning to peel. He went up to the wall and felt it with his hand. The flimsy modern walls had never been to his liking.

Langfuss and his tales. When they took possession of the house, the walls had been newly whitewashed, and that in itself had made him suspicious.

After a time Weiss heard the sound of running, the gate opening and shutting with a bang, and footsteps coming up the garden path. Batsheva opened the door and rushed into the living room, pale and trembling. She screamed with the last of her strength, "Murderer!"

Riva and Chasida came running in alarm to the door.

"Murderer!" repeated Batsheva in a demented shriek. "You're all murderers!"

Weiss looked at Riva and Chasida as if to say, "You see, I was right."

Batsheva rushed into her room and locked herself in. Chasida, completely confounded by this turn of events, hurried after her and knocked on the door, hoping to calm her down. Batsheva did not open the door and when the old woman asked, "Batsheva, what's the matter with you?" she answered from inside the room, "Leave me alone, you make me sick."

No one could remember her crying before. It was astonishing to think of her blue eyes reddened and flowing with tears, her face wet and twisted. Riva remembered one evening when Batsheva lay on her bed and wept, but this time she seemed completely different.

Weiss told them calmly what he had done.

"You've ruined your daughter's life," said Chasida.

"She'll forget this too," said Weiss. "People forget everything."

"Why did you do it?" asked Riva.

"Because he's not religious. I won't stand for my daughter going out with freethinkers. He doesn't even wear a hat."

· 23 ·

BATSHEVA DID NOT RETURN TO WORK. DAY AFTER DAY SHE SAT
in her room and cried. "Where does the girl get the strength
to cry so much?" marveled Chasida. Chasida brought her
meals to her room. Batsheva lay on her bed, dressed in the
clothes she had been wearing on the day she locked herself
in, and did not leave her room. Weiss was not perturbed.
Day and night Batsheva lay and wept, but he said that the
crisis would pass and everything would return to normal.

It was a late, rainy winter. All day the house was shrouded
in gloom, damp and cold. Batsheva lay in bed fully dressed
and wept. Chasida said that the child was killing herself little
by little. But Batsheva was a strong and determined girl.

One day she got out of bed and said, "Enough." She went
into the bathroom, bathed, combed her hair, changed her
clothes, and sat down with them at the table. They behaved
as if nothing out of the ordinary had happened and nobody
asked any questions. In the end Weiss asked, "When do you
intend going back to work?"

Batsheva did not reply. She went on sitting at home and
she did not even go out into the yard or the garden. She
began to talk again. Riva encouraged her, and Batsheva asked
her never to mention that idiotic affair to her again. She
began to smile at her father. Finally she admitted to him that
he had done the right thing, and even begged his pardon for
the sorrow she had caused him. He embraced her and kissed
her, like a father whose long-lost daughter had been returned
to him safe and sound. Once more Batsheva's nervous laughter rang through the house, with Riva aping her. The searches
on top of the bureau in Chasida's room were resumed.

Chasida told Weiss.

"What are you afraid of, Chasida?" he asked. "If you

haven't got any money, they won't find anything. They'll give up and the searches will stop.''

Chasida insisted that it wasn't right. Weiss said that he agreed with her completely, but Chasida was afraid that his love for her was beginning to wane. At night she saw Jerusalem in her dreams, her friends, the Hurva on the Sabbath. Everything was wonderfully clear and vivid. She would lose herself in the narrow arched alleys, weep for her soul before the Western Wall. Waking broke her heart. The mornings were merciless. In her sleep she would beg, Let me sleep a little longer, just a little longer.

The hot weather that set in after Passover fatigued and depressed her. She heard the girls telling their father behind her back about her thefts in the market, about the fortune she was accumulating and hiding from them, and her heart was wrung at Haim Weiss's indifference. The idea of going home began to dominate her thoughts. This was the fantasy with which she consoled herself in her hour of grief. Her wit and caustic tongue no longer evoked an affectionate response from Weiss, and she knew that she was only an old woman. When she emerged from her depression she consoled herself with the thought that at least her future was secure. If Weiss died before she did, she would have to stay with one of the girls—the one who married first—but presumably marriage would cure her of her craziness and she would stop tormenting her. In the depths of her heart, however, she wished that she would die before Weiss. Let him stay with his daughters, she thought. They're his daughters after all, not mine. If only she could have gone for a visit, a few days at least, to Jerusalem. But everyone was talking about the war.

The war was the topic of the day. From time to time Langfuss came and explained. The winter crop was poor. To pay the workers their wages and go on cultivating until the next crop, Weiss wanted to sell part of his big grove.

Langfuss stared at him in amazement. "And who is going to buy an orange grove now?"

Weiss didn't understand.

"At the very most," said Langfuss, "you could get a little money for the land. But who's going to buy land now?"

"Why?"

"Because there's going to be a war."

"And if there is?"

"It will be impossible to send the fruit abroad."

Weiss understood. Now he was glad that he had sold his small groves and bought his big house. The value of this house would always go up, the broker had promised him. But Langfuss did not control the fate of the world, and it was no use blaming him for that. For the time being the war had not yet broken out, and the work of cultivating the grove had to go on.

MASHA WENT ABOUT a lot with Ben-Zioni the overseer. She went about with him until everybody in the colony saw her belly swelling on her long thin frame. And nobody who knew the facts of life imagined that Masha had been made pregnant by the Holy Ghost. Her parents locked her up in the house and would not let her go out, even to work. Her father swore that if he ever laid eyes on Weiss's overseer he would kill him on the spot. Masha said that if he didn't marry her she would kill him herself. But she was locked up in the house and she couldn't kill anybody.

When Ben-Zioni saw which way the wind was blowing, he made himself scarce, disappearing from the colony one fine day with something to help him on his way—the money Weiss had given him to pay the workers' wages. When Weiss heard about it he couldn't believe his ears; he refused to believe that such things were possible. But the bird had flown, his money had flown, there was no overseer in the grove, and the workers were demanding their wages. He took out the cash he had left and paid the workers. Then he fired them. The Arab guard who lived in the grove with his family went on guarding it in exchange for permission to continue living there. Weiss wondered what there was left to guard.

The rent from the house in Train Street could not be counted on to bring in more than small sums, and Weiss's savings were negligible. Chasida was used to poverty and she was not unduly upset at the news of the overseer's flight. The girls did not understand the situation at all and announced that they could not possibly go out to work. Weiss did not argue. Reality will teach them their lesson, he said to himself, and he did not hold it against them.

MASHA'S HOUSE WAS always closed; the windows were kept shuttered in all weathers. A special smell pervaded the house, a sour smell of sweat and bedclothes and fried onions from the kitchen. Weiss's head began to ache from the moment he stepped inside.

"I want to talk to Masha," said Weiss.

Masha's pale, unshaven father sat up in bed, his eyes burning with indignation. Masha's mother sat opposite him on a chair and wept.

"Masha?" said Hershkovitz. "Who's she? We have no daughter of that name in our family."

Weiss understood and said nothing. Masha's mother wiped her eyes on the back of her sleeve and said, "Mr. Weiss, one doesn't mention a rope in the home of a hanged man."

"But when you need the thief, you take him down from the noose," smiled Hershkovitz bitterly, and the bedsprings creaked under his thin body. Mrs. Hershkovitz pressed Weiss to have a glass of tea, but he refused. The very idea made him sick.

"I have to talk to Masha," he said. "He ran away with my money. I want to know where he is."

"He took your money but he left us with a souvenir in her belly," sniggered Hershkovitz.

"Perhaps she knows something about him. I have to find him."

"They say he joined the army," said Masha's mother.

"You didn't go to the police, did you?" said Hershkovitz in alarm.

"No," said Weiss.

"That was good of you, Mr. Weiss," said Masha's mother. "You did us a kindness. You're a decent, honorable man, Mr. Weiss, thank you very much."

"Mr. Weiss," Hershkovitz suddenly shouted, "don't let her come near you, the wicked bitch of a whore. Don't demean yourself by talking to her."

Masha came into the room. Her pregnancy was obvious, her tread heavy. Her eyes were swollen and her feet were bare.

"Where is Ben-Zioni, Masha?" asked Weiss gently. "I need him. He ran away with all my money."

"You wicked girl," said her father. "Tell Mr. Weiss everything or he'll turn us out of the house that you've turned into I don't want to say what. Tell him or I'll throttle you like a dog!"

"It never occurred to me to do such a thing," protested Weiss.

"Never you mind," whispered Hershkovitz into Weiss's ear. "It's to frighten her."

"I don't know anything, Mr. Weiss. On my life I don't know," swore Masha, and spat on the floor.

"You've been lucky with your overseers, Mr. Weiss," sighed Masha's mother with a sad smile.

"Masha's been lucky with his overseers too," said her father.

"Baruch was a decent boy," said Weiss angrily.

"They're all decent boys," said Hershkovitz. "They all want to devour their fellow men decently."

Weiss looked silently at Masha.

"Let the rotten whore get out of here," said Hershkovitz, "and may I never set eyes on her again."

The rotten whore left the room.

"Yehezkiel's a sick, unemployed man," said Masha's mother apologetically. "He's never spoken so rudely in my hearing before. This is the first time. What can we do?" she asked, and began to cry again. "We've never done anybody any harm. We've never owed anyone a penny. Everybody knows us . . ."

"Mr. Weiss has heard that before. And what comes next?" asked Hershkovitz.

· 24 ·

AS THE SUMMER DRAGGED ON, THIN CRACKS BEGAN TO APPEAR on the walls in a number of the rooms in the new house. Weiss cursed modern building and invited Langfuss to come and see "his" house with his own eyes.

"It's nothing," said Langfuss, "cracks in the paint."

When the cracks widened and deepened, Langfuss said, "The land plays tricks here. It's nothing. Cracks in the plaster."

Then the floor tiles began to wobble and tilt on the floor. The plaster on the ceiling began to peel. Langfuss was not perturbed. The war was behind his back, protecting him. He smiled behind the thick lenses of his spectacles, crossed his legs, and said, "And of the men of the Sharon he would say, May it be thy will, Oh Lord our God and God of our fathers, not to turn their houses into their graves—a quotation from the prayer of the high priest on the Day of Atonement, Mr. Weiss."

"The prayers of the Day of Atonement won't stop up the cracks in my house," said Weiss crossly. "Who knows, perhaps we're endangering our lives by living in it. I made a big mistake, Mr. Langfuss, I'm telling you, a big mistake."

"Mistake nothing," said Langfuss calmly. "You have to have repairs done every year, plaster the cracks and paint the walls. The land plays tricks here. Everyone does the same." The thick gold ring glittered on his ring finger and infuriated Weiss.

They were sitting in the garden and Chasida brought them refreshments. The girls stayed inside. Batsheva had not yet ventured out. The trees, the well-watered lawn, and the flowers brought a breath of fresh air. They sat in the dark and they could hardly see each other. Suddenly Riva appeared in the doorway and came and sat down beside them. She sat well back in the chair, crossed her legs like Langfuss, and asked her father if his headache was better. Weiss mumbled something but Riva paid no attention to his reply.

"And you, Riva, how are you feeling?"

"Thank you, Mr. Langfuss," replied Riva, "it could be better and it could be worse."

"Ah, but what is better and what is worse?" said Langfuss smartly.

"I'm tired," she said, exempting herself from the effort of matching the broker's wit in her reply.

Langfuss looked at her and smiled. Riva could not see if the smile was mocking or affectionate.

"Mrs. Chasida," said Langfuss, "why does Riva work so hard all day long that she is tired out when evening comes?"

Chasida narrowed her eyes. "Life is boring without work," she said, and was silent.

"When you already knew that there was going to be a war and the citrus farmers would lose money," said Weiss suddenly to Langfuss, "you urged me to buy more citrus groves."

"I'm not a prophet," said Langfuss.

"But you wouldn't agree to sell even a piece of my grove."

"I don't sell and I don't buy. I'm only a broker."

"Oh, never mind," sighed Weiss. "As long as we're still alive."

"As long as we've got our health," added Chasida, "the rest is unimportant."

"If only everyone was like Chasida," said Weiss, moving his chair closer to hers and putting his arm around her. The old woman felt shy and the glittering gold earrings on her tiny ears trembled beneath her wig. Langfuss stood up. He saw that Riva was looking at him as if she were concealing something, something she wanted to reveal to him.

"Shall we go for a little walk, Riva?" he asked, and Weiss shuddered.

Riva stood up, smoothed down her skirt, and said, "Why not?"

Chasida smiled encouragingly at them. If only Riva was happy, she said to herself, everything would be different.

They walked down Founders Street. They stood between the empty stalls in the marketplace. The empty barrels standing on the pavement gave off a smell of herring.

"It seemed to me that you had something you wanted to say to me," said Langfuss.

"In other words, our little walk is conditional."

"God forbid, I never said that."

When they walked down Train Street, Riva said, "You can embrace me if you like. I'm not made of glass."

Langfuss could not believe his ears. He tried to laugh it off, but then he took his short, plump arm and put it around her waist. "Is that all right?" he said.

"It could be better. It could be worse."

"The worse the better," he said, and he could already see what the rest of the walk was going to be like.

They walked on, crossed the railway tracks, and approached the orange groves.

"Is there no danger from the Arabs?" asked Riva.

"There's no danger from the Arabs," he said, and the lenses of his spectacles misted over in the dew.

"Make up your mind if you're a man or not," demanded Riva, and the words stunned him and fell like heavy stones into his heart.

"What's happened to you, Riva?" he asked. "You don't know what you're saying this evening. I've never known you like this."

"I don't give a damn."

"You sound like Batsheva."

"You're not worthy to mention her name, Langfuss. Don't worry, I won't hurt you."

They sat down on a rock next to one of the orange groves. All around them was a great silence. With one hand he encircled her shoulders and pressed her to his heart, and with the other he stroked her hair and the nape of her neck.

Riva felt his thick spectacles separating them. One of the cold metal earpieces touched her cheek and sent a shiver down her spine. His eyes shone behind the lenses like the eyes of an owl.

"You don't know how to make love," said Riva.

"And you know? Where from? You've never been in love with anyone." But his lips touched her cheek and gradually she sensed that they were getting closer to her mouth.

At that moment she stood up and linked her arm in his, and they continued their walk between the orange groves and the fields, where the smell of the dry dung wafted toward them on the evening breeze.

"Shall we sit down and talk for a while?" asked Riva.

"With pleasure," he replied.

They went into one of the groves and sat down on the steps of an abandoned packing shed.

"Are there any snakes here?" asked Riva. "I'm afraid of snakes."

"There are no snakes here."

"Take your spectacles off."

"What's that got to do with it?"

"They bother me. What do you care? I'm asking you."

"I can't see a thing without them. I'm very shortsighted."

"In any case it's dark and you can't see anything anyway."

"What about you?"

"You can see me without your spectacles."

Riva giggled, and Langfuss's expression grew grave.

"You forget, Riva, that I'm much older than you are. Have you got any idea what we came here for and what we're doing here?"

"Once I asked you to save me, and you pretended not to understand and you didn't answer me."

"I don't remember," he said. "But everyone is preoccupied by his own problems. You should know that."

"It's hard to wait."

"I knew you were suffering, Riva. In your family the suffering screams from the walls."

"The cracked walls," said Riva, and smiled sadly.

"Now you're the real Riva again," said Langfuss. "Simple and unaffected. Forget Batsheva's affectations and be a girl like all the other girls. Listen to my advice, Riva."

He locked the fingers of one hand in hers and stroked her with the other. She felt the warmth of his hairy hand on her arm and elbow. Suddenly he removed his hand, took off his spectacles, and put them in his shirt pocket.

Once more his warm hand came down on her shoulder, slid down her arm, caressing her. His face bent over her neck. She smelled the perspiration around his eyes. His short eyelashes were sticky and they tickled her cheek. His breath warmed her lips in fast, rhythmic pants. She turned her face toward him and his lips groped for her mouth. For a moment she felt their tender flesh, but she quickly averted her face and her mouth landed on his cheek and the side of his nose. He kissed her cheek. His hand stroked her shoulder.

"I told you you weren't a man," she taunted him. "You don't know how to make love. You kiss on the cheek."

He did not answer her. She began to feel revulsion at his shy, fumbling caresses. Suddenly she saw Batsheva lying in her room, reading in the lamplight. Her nightgown was spotless and fragrant, her sheets were starched and immaculate. Her dainty hands held a novel in new brown paper. Her gray-blue eyes ran over the lines. Her face was white and still as a statue.

Suddenly she woke up with a start. The broker's lips slid down her ear, brushed her cheek, and pressed down on her mouth. She closed her eyes tightly and clenched her jaws, but she did not avert her face. When she felt his sweaty hand stroking her breast, she put her hand into his shirt pocket, took out his spectacles, and threw them into the trees.

Langfuss froze. He stared at her, gaping. Riva rose slowly to her feet and tidied her hair and dress. He tried to grab her again but she pushed him away and started walking toward the gate. Langfuss began to groan. He lay down flat on his stomach and began crawling and groping for his spectacles between the trees. When she had gone a little way, she stopped, for she thought she could hear Langfuss crying. Langfuss crying! A sight she did not want to miss. She retraced her steps, stopped a short distance away, and stood looking at him. He was sitting on the ground with his legs folded under him, holding his head in his hands and moaning like a dying animal. The pressure came back to Riva's chest and stomach, and the memory of the taste of his tender lips made her shudder.

Langfuss called her and she did not reply. She looked at him and she knew that he could not see her at all. He sat on the ground and wept. He despaired of finding his spectacles. He wandered blindly through the trees, groping his way in the dark. The pressure in Riva's chest increased and her body froze. She bent over next to a tree and vomited. Langfuss heard and came toward her with his hand stretched out in front of him to protect him from the branches. He reached her, grabbed her sleeve, and clutched her to him. She tried to get away, but he held her body like a vise.

"You're insane!" he exclaimed. "As crazy as your sister and the rest of your family. What did you think? That the jackals would devour poor Langfuss, blind in the orange grove?"

"Langfuss!" shrieked Riva, trying to free herself, and her voice echoed over and over again in the empty distances. He pounced on her and tore off her dress.

When the clock in the Weiss's house struck twelve, Riva had still not come home. Weiss was ill, his eyes were blurred with the dizziness and the pain in his head. He cursed the broker bitterly. Chasida stood at the head of his bed, placing wet compresses on his brow. In the hour of his affliction Weiss's love for Chasida returned.

Batsheva placed a bookmark between the pages of her novel, closed it, and put it down on the bedside table. She switched off the light, pulled the sheet up to her shoulders, and tried to fall asleep. She was still awake when Riva finally came home.

· 25 ·

WHEN HAIM WEISS FELT SOMEWHAT BETTER HE WENT OUT TO his orange grove and tried to put in a little work, as much as he was able, so that all the labor and money he had invested in the grove would not go to waste and he would earn something from the crop, at least on the local market. For the first time in his life he tasted the sensation of physical labor, and it revived his spirits and made him feel as if Baruch his overseer had come back to life. In his old age, with his body weakened by illness and his big house gloomy and decaying, he found some peace in the shade of his fruit trees. The results of his work were meager, but it brought him great relief. Thus he began spending the late summer days in his orange grove. The fruit was already ripe and the yield was not bad considering the neglected state of the grove. Every now and then he would rest and watch the Arab family living in the packing shed curiously. The guard's wife kneaded dough, made a fire, and baked bread.

The picking season approached. Weiss decided to start picking. He borrowed money and hired workers. Everyone shook their heads commiseratingly, but he was determined not to let the fruit rot on the trees.

He managed to sell some of the fruit to the army camps, but the profits were small. Nevertheless he felt a sense of satisfaction. His work in the grove inflamed his imagination, and he would sit there daydreaming for hours, building castles in the air, and making plans that he did not disclose to anyone.

It was a hard winter. The wind tore down trees and the rain filled the roads with mud. Damp spread in the corners of the walls and ceilings and they began to turn moldy. Again Weiss succumbed to fits of vomiting and violent headaches.

Chasida stayed up all night, sitting beside him and waiting for him to speak. He asked her to move his bed into her room, so that she would be close at hand. He knew that when summer came he would go out into the orange grove and he would be well again, but the winter dragged on until after Passover. The rains and the wind did not let up.

Then the days grew fine and warm again. The earth dried quickly and split into deep cracks. The cracks in the walls of the house widened, and here and there the sky was already visible through them.

One evening there were screams from the water tower, and from the garden they could see people running toward the hill. Weiss was lying in bed and he asked Chasida to go and see what had happened. She went out and followed the running people. At the foot of the water tower Masha lay dead. The neighbors said that she was no longer pregnant, but nobody knew if she had given birth at all. Masha had spent the whole year imprisoned in her parents' house, and people seemed to imagine that her pregnancy had continued all that time. Now she lay on the sand, her head smashed in and her brightly colored dress, which the whole colony knew, stained with blood. No one from her family was there. After calling the police everyone hurried home to spread the news of Masha's death.

Chasida was stunned. She had hardly known Masha, but the sight of her death horrified her. Weiss listened to her story indifferently, shook his head, and said nothing. Riva and Batsheva questioned her closely.

In the latter stages of his illness Weiss lost all interest in anything outside his own home. He no longer thought about his grove; he forgot all the plans he had dreamed about in the winter. The money in the house ran out, and Chasida did not dare to ask how she was to pay for their food. The rent from the house in Train Street had not yet been paid, and she was afraid to go there and ask for it. The girls did not even think of going out to work. Batsheva still confined herself to the house. Weiss lay apathetic and remote on his bed. He hardly allowed Chasida to leave him alone in the room.

The summer was hot and humid and she thought of her Jerusalem, which had already been transformed in her imagination into a kind of exotic "Orient." She heard people coming into the garden, a crowd of people speaking in loud voices. She hurried to the window and saw a group of Arab workers on the veranda. One of them banged on the door. She was afraid to go out. Riva opened the door and turned pale. When she tried to go back in and shut the door behind her, they would not let her; they shouted and demanded their wages. They asked to see the old man so that he could pay them right away. Batsheva came out of her room and helped Riva to lock the door. After a moment the banging began again, and they heard the shouts of a number of Jewish creditors too.

Weiss called out from his room to ask Chasida for a glass of tea. Chasida said nothing, but when he finally heard the shouting outside and the panic-stricken whispers of Riva and Batsheva, he suddenly shook off his apathy and asked what was going on.

"Nothing," said Chasida reassuringly. "A few people have come to ask for money."

Weiss did not say anything.

"The Arab workers," continued Chasida, "and a few Jewish moneylenders."

"I don't owe them a penny," announced Weiss.

Batsheva came into the room, pale and trembling.

"I don't owe them a penny," repeated Weiss. "Tell them to go home and stop making a nuisance of themselves."

The people outside kept on knocking at the door. Chasida

was afraid that they would break it down. Batsheva and Riva whispered together. Riva combed her hair, got dressed, and went out through the back door.

All the way she felt as if she were stepping on broken glass. Next to the big synagogue she paused, closed her eyes, and sighed bitterly. Then she crossed the square and stood in front of Langfuss's house. She opened the gate quietly and went in.

His mother opened the door and asked her to wait a moment. Langfuss came into the room, with a new pair of spectacles on his nose and a beaten expression in his downcast little eyes. He did not look at her.

"Mr. Langfuss," her voice choked.

"Yes?"

"The Arab workers . . ."

"Yes, I know."

"My father is ill and I thought . . ."

"Yes. Sit down for a minute. I'll come in a minute," he said.

"No, no, I only meant . . ."

"Yes, I know everything."

His voice was hard and cold. He did not raise his eyes. He kept his hands in his pockets. He put on his hat, took his walking stick, and let her go out in front of him.

"Everything happens so quickly that you don't have time to think," Riva apologized.

"Yes," said Langfuss. "You don't have time to think."

All the way to the house she didn't say a word, and Langfuss too was silent. They went in at the front gate, and they found the veranda deserted. Riva was alarmed and hurried to the house, with Langfuss walking mechanically behind her. The men were already inside Weiss's room and Chasida was trying to get them out.

When they saw Riva coming in with Langfuss behind her, they all gathered round the broker and laid their complaints before him. Langfuss went up to the sick man and reassured him. Weiss was completely oblivious to what was happening around him, and Langfuss saw that he didn't understand a word he, Langfuss, was saying. Suddenly the old man stretched out his hand, took Langfuss's hand, brought it to his mouth, and kissed it.

Langfuss was moved and his eyes misted over. He mumbled something and was unable to hide his emotion.

He got the people out of the room, told them to come and see him in his office, and calmed them down. Nobody knew how much it cost him.

When silence descended on the house again, Chasida began to cry.

"Why are you crying, Chasida? That Langfuss has stolen enough money from me. Let him pay."

She was startled to hear Weiss speaking so lucidly. He sent her a weary smile.

"I'm still waiting for that tea, Chasida. I'm dying of thirst."

"WHAT WERE YOU so scared of, Batsheva?" asked Weiss. "Why did you run and hide in your room? Were you afraid they were going to take you as a hostage?"

Batsheva looked at Chasida and said nothing.

"Leave her alone, Haim," said Chasida. "We were all frightened. I thought they were going to pull the house down around our ears and kill us all."

Batsheva left the room and went to Riva. "It's impossible to talk to him," she said. "Grandma sits there all the time listening."

Riva was pale and depressed.

"You've become a woman," said Batsheva suddenly. "You look like a grown-up woman who knows everything."

"Leave me alone," said Riva.

"Why should I leave you alone? Perhaps you intend allowing him to dispossess us because of that old woman?

You don't do anything, Riva, you wait for me to do all the work myself."

"Let's talk about it tomorrow," begged Riva.

"She's got money, the old woman, I'm sure of it," said Batsheva. "If only I knew where she was hiding it."

"If she had any money she would have given it to us to pay the workers," said Riva.

"She wants to humiliate us, you don't understand," said Batsheva angrily. "If only you could have seen how happy she was when she saw you going to beg favors of Langfuss."

"There's something evil in you, Batsheva, something diabolical that makes you take a peculiar pleasure in hating people and blaming them," Riva burst out.

"And Father?"

"What about Father?" asked Riva.

"Fit as a fiddle. He's perfectly lucid and there's nothing the matter with him. He was only pretending, to make Langfuss feel sorry for him."

"And the way he kissed his hand?"

"A comedy."

Riva was furious. She ran to the old man's room and opened the door. She saw Chasida dozing on the chair and her father lying in bed, his eyes open, his face distorted, and his lips muttering in delirium.

She slammed the door and went back to Batsheva. She looked into her gray eyes with hatred and said, "You bitch!"

At the end of the week Weiss regained consciousness. He asked them not to sell his orange grove. They were all too embarrassed to protest, until Batsheva asked boldly, "Why shouldn't we sell it?"

"Because it's the orange grove that my Baruch looked after for me," sighed Weiss.

He returned to the subject of the house in Founders Street which would pass into the possession of whichever daughter married first, and said that he had put it into his will that

Chasida could stay there as long as she lived. He asked them to make their peace with each other and not to quarrel. Not to torment Chasida. Not to remember him.

After a few days of delirium, he closed his eyes and gave up the ghost.

· 26 ·

CHASIDA UTTERED A TERRIBLE SCREAM, AND THE TWO GIRLS looked at her rebukingly. The doctor packed his bag and left. The door closed behind him and Chasida looked around her as if she had been thrown there out of a dream, as if she had been cast up on the shores of a foreign country.

"His will has no validity. There's no proof that he was of sound mind when he wrote it. And besides, the whole thing is utter madness. It's unheard of," said Batsheva.

"Have a little shame at least, Batsheva," protested Riva. "He's still lying there."

"Old woman," said Batsheva. "Have you seen the will with your own eyes?"

"No, Batsheva, I haven't seen it," mumbled Chasida.

"In that case, it never existed," announced Batsheva. "There never was a will or anything else."

Riva rebuked her.

"You can pack your bags, Grandma," said Batsheva.

Riva removed her sister by force, and Chasida hurried to shut herself up in her room. The dead man remained alone.

Chasida did not pack up her bags, but in the big room at the back of the house she rearranged her belongings which were scattered over the bureau. Then she went back to the dead man's room and dragged her bed back into her room.

She knelt down beside it and began feeling the mattress. Her eyes were dry and her wig was awry on her head. The two amber earrings trembled on her ears and gleamed dully in the electric light.

She stood up and switched off the light. Then she knelt down by the bed again, laid her head on the mattress, and prayed that her punishment would come quickly and save her.

A heavy silence settled on the house. Only the clock in the passage ticked monotonously.

Riva knocked on Chasida's door. Her eyes were red from weeping. "We are alone now, Grandma," she said, "more alone than ever."

"Yes, Riva," sighed the old woman, and rose to her feet. She covered the mattress and stood facing Riva, waiting for her to go on. Riva was silent.

"I see that you are very frightened, Riva," said Chasida finally.

"Yes."

"Because of the dead?"

"Because of the living."

"Well?" asked the old woman impatiently.

"Batsheva intends to sell the orange grove, in spite of his request."

"It's none of my business. The grove is yours."

"She wants to turn you out of the house."

"There is still a law in this world!" cried Chasida.

"But there's no will, you said so yourself."

"I never said that there was no will. I only said that I had never seen it," said Chasida.

"Yes," agreed Riva.

"Why does she want to sell the orange grove?"

"So that we can live on the proceeds."

"Perhaps she's right."

Riva was shocked.

"Perhaps you should lease it," said Chasida.

"Who to?"

"You must ask Langfuss."

Riva blushed, and once again she felt the pressure of the insult in her chest and behind her eyes. She sat down on the old woman's bed.

"I see that you feel bad," said Chasida sympathetically.

"Very bad," said Riva, and she began to cry.

Chasida clasped Riva's head to her bosom and stroked her smooth brown hair. "Cry, it's good for you. I myself could never shed a tear when my loved ones died. Not a single tear. And to this very day I can still feel the pressure of those unshed tears. Even now I can't cry, you can see for yourself. My eyes simply refuse to obey me."

Chasida's hands were scaly but warm. Her clothes gave off a fresh smell of soap. Riva did not remove her head from the old woman's bosom until the latter looked at her and said, "What is Batsheva doing?"

Riva stopped crying and looked up, wrinkling her narrow brow. "I don't know. Why do you ask?"

"Now we are alone, my child. We must stop hating, and try to live together in peace. As he asked us to do."

"You know Batsheva," said Riva.

"I thought I knew you too, and it seems that I was wrong," said Chasida.

"No one could be wrong about her," protested Riva.

"Yes, indeed they could," said the old woman, trying to smile. "Man sees into the eyes, but God sees into the heart."

Riva said nothing. Chasida took her courage in both hands and asked, "Now, Riva, perhaps you will explain why you accused me of stealing? Why did you do it?"

"It was her idea."

"But it was you who conducted the searches."

Riva got up and left the room.

AFTER THE FUNERAL Chasida mourned for the seven days laid down by the Law. During these days the women hardly exchanged a word. When Friedman and Borochov came to pay their respects, the two girls shut themselves up in their rooms.

Friedman sighed, "All the decent and respectable people pass away. Only the drunken cart drivers go on living."

The teacher Borochov looked more embarrassed than usual. He glanced in the direction of the bedrooms, looked at Chasida, and said nothing.

"They are in their rooms," said Chasida.

"No," said Borochov, "I was just thinking."

"What were you thinking about?"

"Weiss was a wonderful man," proclaimed Friedman. "I can still remember when we went to visit him . . ."

"How are Hadassah and the baby?" Chasida interrupted him.

"Well, thank you," said the teacher Borochov. "You promised you would come to visit us. You haven't been to see us once since you arrived in the colony."

"The baby Esther is a big girl already!" remarked Friedman.

The expression on Borochov's face showed that he had come to a decision. He drew his chair closer to Chasida, looked at her and said, "Chasida, we want to help you and we don't know how. Perhaps it would be best if you left this house now and came to live with us?"

"Out of the question," said Chasida firmly. "I feel at home here. I lack for nothing."

"And the girls?" asked Borochov in a whisper.

"They are good to me."

"Have you got any money?"

"Everything is fine. There's nothing to worry about."

"I told you so!" cried Friedman gleefully. "I told you that there was nothing to worry about. He and Hadassah worry about you all the time, and I told them, Chasida knows how to take care of herself. She's got brains."

After the seven days of mourning were over, Chasida went out into the orchard in the back yard, picked the fruit that was growing wild, and sold it in the market. Masha's mother brought the rent. She looked ill; her hair was white and her eyes were swollen.

The cracks in the walls grew wider. The ceiling was full of holes, and Chasida was afraid of the approaching winter. One day little Napoleon, who had been apprenticed to a builder, came and examined the walls with his bleary eyes. He felt them with an expert hand and delivered his verdict in one word: "Renovate."

Chasida agreed. "Renovate, do whatever you like, as long as we're not flooded out in the winter."

For a week Napoleon scraped around the cracks, removed the plaster, replastered the holes, and steadied the tiles. The house was full of dark stains. Then he brought a pail full of whitewash and whitewashed the stains. The house resumed its former appearance and little Napoleon received his wages from Chasida, to the astonishment of Riva and Batsheva.

Once again the whispering began, the hints about the stealing in the marketplace, the money that she was hoarding. Her room was searched. Riva no longer looked on her kindly, as in the days of mourning. When they sat down to eat they would ask her where she had bought the vegetables, where the fruit, and when she paused in confusion or embarrassment before she replied, they would smile knowingly and threaten that they would go to the market to return the stolen goods to their rightful owners.

Batsheva did not leave the house at all. Riva's excursions were short and rare. From the day of Haim Weiss's death

Langfuss had not come to their house, and at the funeral too they had not seen him. Even during the days of mourning he had not come to pay his respects to them. But Riva did not hold it against him.

One evening there was a knock at the door. Riva went to open it. In the doorway stood Shor the Monk. He peered at her out of his mane of red hair. Riva did not ask him in.

"Is this Weiss's house?" he asked.

Riva was disconcerted and called Chasida. The old woman asked him what he wanted.

"I've come to visit Haim Weiss," said Shor.

The two women paled and stiffened. He burst inside and began prowling from room to room, crying, "Mr. Weiss, Mr. Weiss! I've come to beg your forgiveness!"

Batsheva, as usual, immediately shut herself up in her room. He knocked on her door, claiming that Weiss was in there hiding from him. "Open up, Mr. Weiss," he called loudly and clearly. "Open up. I've come to beg your pardon."

"There's no one in there," said Riva.

"Where is Mr. Weiss?" demanded the Monk.

Chasida said to him, "Sir, don't you know that Mr. Weiss departed this world over a year ago?"

"The Day of Atonement is coming," said the Monk, "and I have to obtain Mr. Weiss's forgiveness."

"Mr. Weiss is dead," screamed Riva. "Leave us alone, you madman, get out of our house!"

The Monk opened his eyes wide. "Dead? Haim Weiss? How can that be?"

"Go away, you lunatic," begged Riva, "go somewhere else."

"A catastrophe!" cried Shor. "A catastrophe! Haim Weiss is dead! The crown of our heads has fallen . . ."

He ran off in great agitation and continued shouting in the street, "May the memory of the righteous be blessed and

the name of the wicked perish! Charity will save us from
death . . .''

· 27 ·

BATSHEVA EMERGED FROM HER ROOM, COMPOSED AND ELE-
gantly dressed, sat down at the dining room table, and waited
for the meal to be served. Riva looked at her in astonishment,
still out of breath from the terrifying appearance of the Monk.

"I don't know that man," sighed Chasida.

"She doesn't know that man," said Batsheva in a neutral
voice.

Riva sat down at the table without saying a word, and
Chasida began dishing up their supper.

"We must go and speak to Langfuss about the grove,"
said Batsheva. "And don't start telling me what father said.
I know it as well as you do."

"I'm not going to him," said Riva.

"You'll go, Riva, and how you'll go," said Batsheva and
smiled.

"We'll see."

"I'll go, children. Perhaps I should go," suggested Chasida.

"*You'll* go?" Batsheva opened her gray eyes wide and
stared at her. Chasida understood and fell silent.

"*You* had better pack your bags and go back to where you
came from, Grandma. Everything's over now, Grandma, understand? Everything's over," said Batsheva.

"You haven't married yet, Batsheva," retorted Chasida.
"You're not mistress of this house yet."

"And who is mistress of the house?" asked Riva.

"As God is my witness, I don't know," said Chasida.

Riva was furious. Her eyes clouded with rage. "Are you going to steal our house from us too?"

"Riva . . ." begged Chasida.

"Isn't it enough that we can't show our faces in the street because of the disgrace you've brought upon us with your stealing in the marketplace, but now you want to turn us out of our home as well?"

"Tell me, Grandma, why have you wormed your way into our lives? What are you doing in our house? We don't even know you. Please, leave us alone and go back to your own house. You won't be sorry, I promise you. After all, you'll leave us and go back to Jerusalem with a great fortune."

Chasida bowed her head. "After all I've done for you, for your father, for this house . . ."

"Do you want to be paid for it?"

"No, I don't want anything. All I want is for you to show a little consideration for an old woman."

"Go to Friedman," suggested Batsheva.

"Thank you," replied Chasida, "thank you both very much."

She rose from the table without finishing her food and went to her room. She sat there for a long time until Riva knocked at the door. She opened the door and Riva came in and locked the door behind her.

"Don't listen to her," whispered Riva. "Stay here. Don't give in to her. You have as much right to stay in this house as she does. There's room for all of us."

WHEN CHASIDA GOT UP early in the morning to go to the market, she imagined that the storm had spent itself and that they would leave her alone for a while, until a new storm blew up. On her way home she dropped in at the Langfusses'. Langfuss's mother told her that her son was not at home, but she had heard him talking to his mother before she knocked at the door.

She took her leave of the widow Langfuss and walked up Founders Street. In front of the house, on the lawn, she found all her belongings stacked in a pile. For a moment she stood there aghast, and the heavy baskets of vegetables fell from her hands. Then she recovered herself and began putting her things back in her room. She made the bed and arranged her things on top of the bureau. She stroked her old mattress.

That night the tears came gushing out. All night long she wept, and in the morning she informed them that she was going back to Jerusalem.

Batsheva said that she had better go soon, before the winter.

She began collecting her belongings. Batsheva helped her. When everything was standing packed and ready outside, and the two girls were standing in the door to say goodbye, she began to cry again. She picked up her bundles and returned them to the house, saying in the middle of her tears, "And who will look after you when I'm gone? The two of you will die of hunger alone."

"She's making fun of us, Riva," said Batsheva. "She's putting on a comedy for our benefit." She looked at the old woman and added, "Our father was a strong, healthy man all his life."

"The doctor said that he died of a heart attack," said Riva.

"He had a strong heart, I know it," insisted Batsheva.

"Ah," sighed Chasida, "we all have to die in the end."

"When she was sitting in his room all day and night," said Batsheva, "I was afraid. I was very afraid, but I never imagined how far she would go, this old woman."

"She poisoned him," said Riva.

"Riva, Riva!" cried Chasida.

"Hold your tongue," said Batsheva. "We know everything. Don't worry, we're not going to hand you over to the police. We have to think of the honor of the family."

AFTER A TIME Chasida packed her bags again. It was raining and the roads were full of mud. Once more the two girls stood in the doorway to say goodbye. Batsheva waved a white handkerchief; she even pretended to be crying and wiped her eyes with it.

Chasida stood in the garden with the rain beating down on her between the branches of the trees. Her wig was soaked with rain and it began to drip. She stood there for a long time and all her bundles got wet. Finally she picked them all up again, hoisted her old mattress onto her shoulders, and returned to the house. She hung up her things to dry, took off her bedraggled wig, and walked around the house with her shaven head in her wet clothes.

They had never seen her without her wig on before. There was something horrifying in the sight of the shaven head with its gray and white stubble, like the head of a bald old man. Chasida saw the horror in their eyes and covered her head with a clean white kerchief. But the girls avoided her and they wouldn't even sit down at the table with her. She never put her wig on again, and the two little amber earrings peeped out incongruously from underneath the plain white kerchief. The next day she took off the earrings too and hid them in her mattress.

THAT NIGHT CHASIDA burned with fever. Her hands gripped the mattress and one thought hammered in her head—to keep her situation from the ears of the Friedmans. In the morning she did not get up to do the housework. Riva came into her room and asked her how she was feeling. Chasida did not reply, but her body shook beneath the blankets. Riva stood looking at her sadly, and then she went to make her a glass of tea.

"Thank you very much, Riva," whispered Chasida. "You're a good girl in spite of everything."

Riva went on standing opposite her.

"You know, Riva," continued Chasida, "on the Day of Atonement you and your sister sat and ate in front of me on purpose to upset me. You knew that I was fasting and you shouldn't have done such a thing."

Riva left the room without a word. All that day Chasida lay alone, no food or drink passed her lips and no one came into her room. In the evening her fever rose, she lay delirious in her bed, and everything around her grew misty. Her nose and throat were blocked. Her coughing shook the walls. Before dawn she managed to get up and make herself something to eat. In the corridor she encountered Batsheva and she tried to evade her. But Batsheva barred her way.

"What's the matter, Grandma?" she asked in a confidential whisper.

"It's nothing, Batsheva, it will pass," she sighed and tried to get past her.

"Of course it will pass," said Batsheva. "You'll outlive the pair of us. You'll bury us all, and the house will be yours."

Outside the rain poured down. The holidays had come and gone. Chasida prayed for the punishment she knew she deserved, and at night she wrung her hands and begged God to forgive her for her sins. In her dreams she saw herself celebrating the holidays at home in Jerusalem. But she always woke up in a panic, bathed in perspiration. In her dreams, her bundles were outside and she could do nothing to save them. They were getting wet in the rain, drowning in the puddles in the garden, sending up bubbles of air, growing moldy, and all she had left was the mattress she was lying on, the mattress she had brought with her from Jerusalem and treasured like the apple of her eye. She would take her punishment alone, all alone. She did not want anyone to see. Friedman the drunk rolled in the gutter and

Hadassah and Borochov caressed her little sister, the baby Esther, her baby sister who had died. The house had fallen into wrack and ruin and been repaired, and now the walls and ceilings were disintegrating again. Soon they would peel and grow moldy and everything would have to be repaired again by next summer. In the morning she lay in bed, dazed and exhausted. The sky was clear, the wagtails hopped on her window sill, and the sun shone softly. The trees shed the last drops of the night, and everything was bright and dazzling.

Chasida tried to get up, but she did not have the strength and she fell back into bed. She had always kept herself and everything around her scrupulously clean, and now she couldn't even get up to go to the toilet. For a moment the fog cleared and she began to weep soundlessly, her lips quivering as if in prayer. A stinking wetness spread around her and her body shuddered in disgust. Afterward everything went dark and there was no need for her to think any more.

THE TALL, SILVER-HAIRED figure of the widow Langfuss strode up the garden path. At the door she paused for a moment before knocking with the tips of her ringed fingers. She wore a dark, elegant dress which reached almost to her ankles.

Riva opened the door and was overcome with alarm. It was a long time since anyone had visited their house, and the widow Langfuss had always frightened and embarrassed her with her deep, bespectacled eyes and thick black eyebrows, like those of her son.

The widow Langfuss inspected the house with a superior expression, lifting her skirt slightly as if she was afraid of getting it dirty, and tapped the floor with the umbrella that served her as a cane, as if she were searching for buried treasure with a magic wand. Riva ushered her into the salon. Batsheva, who was reading a novel, closed it immediately and was about to go and shut herself in her room. But the widow Langfuss pointed to the chair with the tip of her umbrella, commanding her to come back and sit down. The three women sat in a strained silence.

"How are you?" asked the widow in a dry voice.

Riva and Batsheva nodded their heads politely.

"Where is the old woman?" she asked.

The girls pointed nervously in the direction of Chasida's bedroom.

"That is for the best," pronounced Mrs. Langfuss.

"We are not responsible for her actions," said Batsheva. "We hardly ever leave the house, and whatever she does, she does of her own accord, out of a mental aberration, but it's not our responsibility . . ."

The widow interrupted her with an impatient gesture.

"All that does not interest me," she said. "Young Langfuss is going out of his mind."

Riva turned pale.

"He has hired workers to do the picking in your orange grove. You are neglecting your own property."

"Is it the picking season now?" asked Riva.

"Before our father died," said Batsheva, "Mr. Langfuss was of great assistance to us."

"In any case the grove is standing abandoned. Why shouldn't he take advantage of it?" said Riva.

"Exactly what I said to him," said the widow, "but he intends giving the proceeds from the crop to you! He's just like his father, he gets these sudden fits of charity and benevolence, but this time he has gone too far! He doesn't care if he loses everything and brings disgrace down on the head of his old mother."

Riva said nothing and Batsheva giggled and looked strangely into the old woman's eyes.

"And you agree to this?" continued the widow. "Why don't you try to talk him out of it? I don't begrudge you, I remember poor Mr. Weiss . . . We all have to die one day, but until that day comes we have to live, no? And he is wasting all my money. Yes, my money, it's all in my name. My late husband's doing. For the sake of convenience, in case of emergencies, you understand . . ." She smiled at them with a conspiratorial air. "You can talk him out of it. Surely you wouldn't want him to waste his mother's money."

"We can't do anything," said Batsheva.

"What do you mean?" asked the widow Langfuss. "He intends giving the money to you!"

"And so?" said Riva crossly.

"And so, you'll tell him what you think of the whole affair. I know you, I know you wouldn't touch a stranger's money, money that doesn't belong to you but to an old widow who only wants to spend what's left of her life in decent respectability."

Chasida suddenly groaned loudly from her room, and the widow Langfuss stood up in alarm. She lifted the hem of her long black skirt, tapped her umbrella on the passage floor, and left without saying goodbye.

"I'm packing my belongings, Riva," mumbled Chasida deliriously, "I'm leaving, I'm going home."

"What's the matter with you?" said Riva.

"I caught cold when I was standing outside in the rain."

Chasida turned her face to the wall and her open eyes emptied.

Riva screamed and Batsheva hurried into the room.

"Blessed be the True Judge," sighed Batsheva. "Close her eyes, Riva."

"I'm afraid," said Riva.

Batsheva went up to the old woman's bed, bent over her, and closed her eyes. She turned to the bureau, swept up all the shabby old bags, and began to open them one by one, turning out the linings as she did so. Then she opened the wet moldy bundles. Riva stood watching her in silence. Finally Batsheva turned the old woman's body over and began to rummage in her clothes.

"Doesn't it disgust you to do that?" asked Riva.

"No," said Batsheva. "There's no difference at all."

An appalling stench rose from the bed. Riva choked and was overcome by giddiness. Batsheva rummaged in her clothes and found nothing. She pulled the sheet off the mattress and the amber earrings gleamed through one of the seams. Batsheva immediately unpicked the seam, pulled out the earrings, and threw them on the floor.

She went on ripping the seam open, and when the hole was large enough she pushed her hand into the stuffing of the mattress. Suddenly her eyes lit up, and Riva shuddered. Batsheva began pulling bundles of banknotes wrapped in newspaper out of the mattress. Bundles and bundles of notes, some old and some new. She heaped them up on the edge of the bed, behind Chasida's dead body, until there was a big pile.

Riva dropped onto a chair and watched Batsheva arranging the banknotes on the bed, presumably the way she had learned to do it in the bank, until her hand came out of the mattress empty.

Batsheva smiled triumphantly.

"You were right again," sighed Riva. "You're always right, you bitch," she said and walked out of the room. After a while Batsheva too left the room, locking the door behind her. Riva was waiting for her in the corridor.

"What are you going to do with her?"

"Tell the Burial Society to come and take her away."

"Wouldn't it be better to tell Friedman?"

"As you wish."

But Riva did not dare. Batsheva hid the bundles of banknotes in the chest in the salon, locked it, and put the key in the empty candy box in the sideboard. When she was finished, she pointed to the chest and said, "You see."

"Where did she get all that money from?" asked Riva.

Batsheva tapped her temple with the middle finger of her right hand and smiled enigmatically.

There was a knock at the door again.

"We're busy today," said Riva.

Langfuss hurried in with an agitated air.

"Was she here?"

"Yes," replied Batsheva.

"Don't listen to her. She doesn't know what she's talking about. She didn't understand my intentions at all. I intended giving you the profits from the crop. There's a demand for fruit in the country again. I was sorry to see the fruit rotting on the trees. So I hired workers, and you'll get the profits after I've deducted my investment. I won't even take a penny for my trouble."

"That's exactly what your mother said," explained Riva.

"What?" said Langfuss in consternation. "Is that what she said?"

Batsheva smiled understandingly.

"I don't understand anything," complained the broker.

"Neither do I," said Riva.

"Chasida is dead," said Batsheva quietly.

Langfuss took off his hat and said, "Blessed be the True Judge."

"She's in her room," continued Batsheva.

"Should I send for a doctor?" asked Langfuss.

"The Burial Society," said Batsheva.

"As far as the orange grove is concerned," mumbled Langfuss, "I didn't want to bother you with the details. I knew that you would agree . . ."

"That's quite all right, Mr. Langfuss," smiled Riva.

"But what did she want here? She always imagines that people are injuring her."

He put on his hat and fled.

Later Friedman and the teacher Borochov came and went

into the old woman's room. After some time they emerged with angry expressions on their faces and left without saying anything to the girls.

Once the body had been removed, Batsheva locked the room and they never went into it again.

AFTER THE PICKING was over, Langfuss brought the girls a tidy sum of money. Riva tried to make up to him with fawning words of thanks, but he made haste to get out of the house.

In the colony people said that Langfuss and his mother quarreled so loudly that the whole street could hear. Langfuss looked gloomy; his eyes were sad and nervous. People said that his mother even hit him.

After the harvest the days were dry. The stains on the walls dried up. A strong smell of mold pervaded the house. The land went on playing its tricks; new cracks appeared. The whitewash flaked off and lumps of plaster fell to the floor. The tiles wobbled under their feet.

· 28 ·

THE WIDER THE CRACKS IN THE WALLS GREW, THE BIGGER THE house seemed to them and the less at home they felt in it. Nobody looked after the orchard or the garden any more. They were overgrown with weeds and thorns.

Riva undertook the housework, which was not much, consisting mainly of preparing meals for herself and her sister. For the sake of convenience they began to take their meals in the kitchen with the two sinks, where they spent most of their time. Riva would go into the colony to do the shopping and the essential chores and Batsheva, true to her vow, never left the house.

Now that the two of them were alone in the big house, Batsheva's thoughts turned again to Nachum Shlomi. It had all happened a long time ago, but she imagined that it had happened yesterday and that the passage of time separating them was an empty vacuum. At first she took Riva into her confidence, describing his body and his ways in great detail, and Riva was ashamed.

The midday scene at the bank floated before her eyes. Nachum Shlomi held out his hand to her father, smiling his friendly smile, and the old man spat in his face. He thought the treacherous Batsheva had sent her father to shame and humiliate him after having deluded him into thinking that she was in love with him. A wound opened in his heart that would never heal. His thin face and gentle eyes were contorted in an expression of sorrow and insult. The most attractive expression for a man—manly strength humiliated, noble and wounded.

Riva listened absentmindedly and Batsheva suspected that her sister did not believe her.

"THERE'S NOBODY LEFT but the two of us now," said Riva. "Each of us for herself and for her sister."

"For her sister and herself," corrected Batsheva with a smile.

Batsheva never gets any older, said Riva to herself. Time leaves no marks on her. Now she's started stirring up the memory of all kinds of dead things, reviving them in her mind. She hasn't changed at all from the day we arrived in the colony, or perhaps I don't notice the changes in her because of my closeness to her.

They had a great deal of money and the future held no fears for them; in fact, it did not exist at all.

Batsheva moved into her father's room. His bed was as it had been on the day of his death, and she did not even change the sheets.

Riva began to suffer from attacks of breathlessness, and she decided to get out of the house a bit and look for work in the colony. But Batsheva's affronted looks discouraged Riva. One evening Langfuss came to visit them and behaved with great affability. Riva offered to pay back the money he had given the workers and debtors before her father's death, but Langfuss refused, saying it was a debt of honor he owed the departed. He told them that the war was over, but they were unmoved by the news. When he said that they should start cultivating the orange grove again, they agreed to lease it to a citrus company.

"That way we won't have to sell the grove," said Riva.

"It was our father's wish," noted Batsheva.

"Yes," said Langfuss. "The main thing is that the war's over."

Riva could not sleep at night. Every project that occurred to her collapsed after a moment's thought. One day when Langfuss came to visit them, she took her courage in both hands and asked him if he would like to go for a walk with her. The memory of their first walk had already faded from her mind. When they stood up to go, Batsheva barred their way and said, "Mr. Langfuss, you should marry Riva. If she marries you, she will receive this house and I will have to be content with the hovel in Train Street."

Langfuss was upset. He didn't understand what she was getting at, or perhaps he pretended not to understand.

"That was our father's will," said Batsheva. "The first to marry gets this house."

"Batsheva," implored Langfuss. "Why do you say such things? After everything I've done for you and your sister!"

"Without asking us. Who asked you to do anything?"

"Batsheva," begged Riva, pale and breathless.

"I think that she is going to have an attack," said Batsheva sadly.

"What's wrong with her?" asked Langfuss.

"It happens all the time," said Batsheva.

"Don't you feel well, Riva?" asked Langfuss.

"No," confessed Riva, and fell into a chair.

Batsheva led the submissive Riva into her room. Langfuss took his leave and hurried off as if he were afraid of being infected by a contagious disease.

The next morning Riva felt better and her breathing returned to normal. Batsheva persuaded her to rest and not to excite herself.

The longer the summer lasted, the more the cracks in the walls widened. They saw that Chasida's repairs had not helped, and there seemed no point in attempting to repair the walls again.

In the winter rain began to drip into the rooms. The long winter nights in the big damaged house filled Riva with fear. Batsheva told Riva that she could come and share the bed in her room, which was still quite sound. At first Riva was repelled by her father's sheets and blankets, but in the end she snuggled up to Batsheva and the warmth of her younger sister's body relieved her fear and distress a little.

Her short excursions into the colony to buy provisions were a painful ordeal to Riva. She would come home short of breath, nervous and frightened. In the winter nights they went to bed early, and Batsheva spoke dreamily about Nachum Shlomi and went into detail about their lovemaking. Riva listened silently, absentmindedly. But Batsheva scarcely noticed her sister's reactions. The figure of Nachum Shlomi had come alive again inside her. She compared his lovemaking with the teacher Borochov's clumsiness and incompetence, laughing scornfully and going into lengthy analyses.

"Father didn't do what he did out of spite," said Batsheva, "but out of his love for me."

"Strange," said Riva.

"Strange but true," insisted Batsheva. "He was simply jealous. The truth is that Father was a child. When he went to the bank he only wanted to see him, but when he saw his wonderful smile, his noble, delicate face, his shapely body, he was overcome by pain and jealousy and so he did what he did. In the last analysis, he had as much right to me as anyone else."

"You're mad," said Riva.

Batsheva wrapped her arms around her sister's neck and warmth spread through Riva's body. "You're a baby," said Batsheva. "You don't know anything about life."

"You imagine, Batsheva, that everyone is a baby compared with you. Either a baby or insane."

Batsheva said nothing. She turned over onto her side and fell asleep. Outside the wind knocked on the shutters. It seemed to Riva that people were prowling around in the orchard and garden, crowds of people like a swarm of invading locusts intent on destroying everything.

The wind knocked on the shutters and tried to get in. Riva almost got up to open the windows. Passionately the wind pressed against the shuttered windows, the winter wind, wild and desperate, beating with its fists and scratching with its nails, whining and howling. From the crack in the corner of the ceiling the raindrops fell monotonously into the pail that Batsheva had placed on the floor to catch them.

· 29 ·

HER DRUNKEN FATHER WILL NEVER DIE, THOUGHT BOROCHOV TO himself, and we'll be stuck here forever in this damp, dreary dullness, this sweet, seething grayness.

A fine spring morning peeped into the teacher Borochov's window. The Passover vacation had just begun, the mornings were bathed in sunshine, the last rain was not yet dry. Hadassah had taken the baby with her to the market, and the first provocative caress of the spring made him feel nervous and depressed.

He was late rising, his face unshaven and his eyes bleary with sleep. I have to get away from here, he thought. Put everything behind me and begin again somewhere else. This was the message that every spring brought to the teacher Borochov. Once more he said to himself, If only I were a poet . . .

He suddenly jumped up and ran to open all the windows wide. From the old man's room the usual stench rose, and his bed was filthy and rumpled. Since the birth of the baby Hadassah no longer took such devoted care of her father. The whole house was flooded with sunshine, fresh scents, and the sound of the chirping of the birds from the garden. Borochov rubbed his eyes and the black stubble on his cheeks and looked out at the big garden. He went into the bathroom, took off his pajama top, and looked sorrowfully at his smooth, plump body, his bloated belly. He opened the tap and looked into the mirror: his upper lip drooping lazily over its sister, his eyes, the deep, black child's eyes that had grown watery, the wrinkles around them. The water flowed into the basin and the teacher Borochov's face in the mirror was flushed, pink and embarrassed. He cupped the water in his hands and began splashing it over his body and face. He took the almond soap and began soaping his chest and armpits. His trousers got wet, but he took no notice.

He woke from his daydream and patted himself dry slowly with a towel. He went back to his room and took clean clothes from the wardrobe, the smell of almond soap enveloping him like a cloud of incense. He left the house and turned onto Founders Street. The front of Weiss's house was shockingly neglected. The thorns had grown to the top of the concrete fence and the entire garden was covered with couch grass. Wildflowers grew around the bottom of the fence and the house looked shut up and deserted.

"Perhaps they're dead," he muttered to himself, and then tittered in embarrassment. He went on walking to the water tower, then he walked back again and lingered for a few minutes outside the house, without daring to go inside. He spent a long time pacing up and down the street, luckily encountering hardly anyone. Shortly before lunchtime he went home.

The festival of Passover was approaching. Hadassah and the maid took all the dishes and the furniture out into the garden. She smiled at him apologetically and asked him if he would mind taking the baby out for a walk. Every morning and afternoon he took the little girl for a walk to Founders Street. They would climb the hill to the water tower and then climb down again and stand opposite Weiss's house. The little girl was quiet and submissive, like her mother, but she looked like her grandfather.

During the week of Passover he went on taking the little girl for daily walks. One day when he was standing next to the water tower hill, he saw Riva emerging with a basket in her hand, bound for the market. He immediately took Esther by the hand and hurried to the house. Batsheva opened the door in astonishment. She stared at him inquiringly with her offended blue eyes.

He sat the little girl down in the living room and led Batsheva into the bedroom.

"What is it?" she asked, pale with dread.

"Nothing, Batsheva," he said, and looked at her fearfully, his upper lip trembling.

"What do you want, Borochov?"

"My Batsheva," he said, "you wouldn't understand."

"Explain yourself. I haven't got all day."

He went up to her and stroked her thin arm. She recoiled in disgust. His eyes narrowed.

"All the time that has passed since that evening in Train Street doesn't exist for me," he said emotionally. "I still love you. I never stop thinking about you."

"I have forgotten everything," she said. "Thank goodness. It's better that way."

"I want to make love to you, Batsheva, even if only for a moment, so as not to forget."

He stretched out his arms to her. She retreated, but her panic and pallor disappeared. Her eyes smiled in cold understanding.

"Borochov," she said, "you'd better leave. Esther is waiting for you in the living room and she might break something."

He did not reply and sat on the bed. Batsheva began to lose patience.

"How disgusting," she said. "You use perfume. The smell of your cheap perfume is all over the house."

"I want to make love to you," he groaned, and tried to grab her. She evaded his hands but she did not leave the room.

"Then, on that evening, you loved me."

"You fool. You must have been blind to think so."

"I know that you loved me. I was the first one, I know I was. You'll love me now too, I'm sure of it, Batsheva. I can't find any peace without you. I walk around in a daze the whole day long."

"Wonderful, Borochov," said Batsheva. "You talk like a poet. Tell me, did you compose those words yourself or did you read them somewhere?"

He was insulted. He buried his head in his lap.

"I'm suffering agonies, Batsheva," he said.

"Stop feeling so sorry for yourself. It's disgusting."

"I don't feel sorry for myself. I hate myself."

"With good reason," she sneered.

"Just let me see your body," he begged feverishly.

"Riva will be back in a moment."

"I don't care," shouted the teacher Borochov. He knelt on the floor and announced that he would not budge.

Batsheva still did not leave the room. She gave him a look of exasperated pity, as if she had resigned herself to the inevitable.

"I'll go out of my mind," he moaned. "I'll go mad. Can't you understand?"

She stood next to him and let him stroke her knee. Her coldness did not seem to put him off. "Go and get undressed," he said.

"I'm not used to such language, Borochov."

"Neither am I," he confessed. "Forgive me."

"Yes, I know," she said, "the summer is coming."

"But here in your house it's always winter, eh? The summer never penetrates your hearts."

"I think that's enough," she said. "Have you calmed down now?"

"Cruel woman."

"I can't stand this any more," she suddenly cried. "Can't you understand? I can't take any more."

"Cruel woman," he whispered in her ear, and began to fondle her. She drew away and opened the door wide. Borochov did not move from his kneeling position on the floor. She raised her hand and pointed at the door. He stared at her lovingly and did not react.

"I can't possibly get up now," he said.

"Try and see," she said.

"It's impossible, I tell you."

She turned on her heel and left the room. He moved to the bed. The front door opened and Riva walked in. Borochov sat rigid on the bed. Then he pulled himself together and got up, walked out of the room, took his little girl, and rushed out of the house.

He hurried down Founders Street, afraid to look behind him. Esther tripped and stumbled as she tried to keep up with his long strides. The midday sun beat down on his head. A handful of Jews were standing outside the small synagogue. The child asked him to stop and rest. He picked her up and carried her.

From her house Nechama screamed, "Thieves! Robbers! Murderers!"

"HE DIDN'T TOUCH ME," said Batsheva.

"I don't care," said Riva.

"I loathe him."

"You don't have to apologize to me."

"But you must believe me."

"I'm not prepared to discuss it any further."

"Riva," said Batsheva, "he's absolutely mad."

"You're surrounded by madmen. Babies and madmen."

"What are you so afraid of?"

Riva did not reply.

"Are you afraid that he'll leave his wife and child to marry me and get this ruin as a prize?"

"You won't succeed in throwing me out in any case."

"It never even occurred to me."

"And I won't live here on sufferance and charity like a poor relation either."

"You're full of hate. Where did you get so much hate from?"

"We'll both rot here, Batsheva. Both of us together, like Chasida. Like two dry sticks."

"Father's last words to me were about his fears for your sanity. He saw the seed of madness in you and suspected that it would develop. He suspected right. He had a discerning eye, did Father."

"You won't frighten me, Batsheva. I'm used to it already. You won't succeed with me. The important thing is to keep cool, not to lose control, to carry on as usual."

After a short silence Riva added, "What you did to Chasida you won't do to me."

"What did I do to Chasida?" Batsheva flared up. "Wasn't I right? Was the money hers?"

"The whole thing was too good to be true."

"Explain yourself, Riva. Tell me all the things you think about me, all the things you've been hiding from me all these years. Hurry up and get it off your chest, Riva, before you have a fit."

"I said that I don't believe all those stories about Chasida."

"And the money?"

"I don't know. Maybe you put it there yourself." Batsheva paled and trembled with rage and astonishment.

"Riva, for God's sake, listen to what you're saying. Tell me yourself if you're sane. Where would I get the money from? Why should I put it in her mattress to incriminate her? Why do you think she was so attached to her mattress that she brought with her from Jerusalem? And whenever she announced that she was leaving she tied it to her bundles and dragged it outside? How can you talk such nonsense? Riva, Riva, what's happening to us? And all because of that revolting Borochov!"

"May he rot in hell," hissed Riva through her teeth. "May he rot in hell with all his family, his little girl and his Hadassah and his drunken father-in-law and their Chasida. I'm sick, Batsheva, perhaps you're right."

Batsheva embraced her and led her to their room, where she made up the bed.

"But it's still afternoon," said Riva.

Batsheva lay down to sleep.

"We haven't even eaten yet," protested Riva. "The baskets are standing full of food in the kitchen."

· 30 ·

THE SUMMER CAME AND THE PLASTER FELL OFF THE WALLS IN showers. The cracks deepened and the ceiling was almost bare above the walls. At night they would hear the sound of an explosion and they would know that another layer of plaster had fallen. It seemed to them that they were safer in their father's room, but Riva was still afraid. She would pull the sheet over her head to protect herself.

That summer the municipal engineer of the colony knocked on their door. He sat in the living room, looked up at the disintegrating ceiling with a worried expression on his face, and asked them what they intended doing about it.

Batsheva said that they hadn't decided yet.

"Look for yourselves," he said. "You can see the iron sticking out of the concrete."

"Yes," said Riva, "we were deceived by the persón who sold us this house."

"There's no question of deceit here," explained the engineer. "It happens all over. The land plays tricks here in the summer when it dries and shrinks after expanding in the winter. The walls and foundations are not so flexible . . ."

"But what can we do?" asked Batsheva.

"Miss Weiss," said the engineer, "you must leave this house. Or pull it down and build a new one in its place. I have to inform you that your lives are in danger in this house."

He stopped and looked at them compassionately.

"I know that you are two girls alone here in this house, but someone must help you. You don't want to be buried alive here under the rubble. This house is too big for you. You can sell the plot and buy a smaller and stronger apartment."

"That is impossible," pronounced Batsheva quietly.

"I'm sorry," said the engineer. "I have brought with me an order warning you to evacuate this house. At least until the beginning of winter."

They opened the door and let him out. The front garden was overgrown with a tangle of tall thorns. The engineer knocked on the door again.

"These thorns must be cleared away immediately," he said. "They can cause fires and attract snakes."

"Is that a municipal ordinance too?" asked Batsheva.

"Yes, that's a municipal ordinance too," said the engineer, and went on his way.

Riva said, "We have been neglecting the house lately."

Batsheva sighed. "Everything is against us, Riva. We must be on our guard. You must take care of your health and we must both hang on. We must be good to each other."

"You're starting again, Batsheva, I can't stand it when you talk like that. As if we were going to die or the world was about to fall apart or something."

"If you prefer to go on dreaming, do so by all means," said Batsheva. "I prefer to look at the world with my eyes wide open." Two frozen lakes lapped the lashes of her wide-open eyes, and her sharp-chinned, triangular face closed in on itself and grew remote.

After the Sabbath someone came from the municipality and served them with a notice to clear the thorns from the garden and orchard immediately. Riva asked them to send a laborer to do the job.

In the morning an Arab youth appeared in the yard with a hoe over his shoulder. Despite the heat he was wearing a dark jacket over his undershirt and the khaki trousers that were too big for him. His face was swarthy and gleaming, smooth but for the downy black mustache and wispy side-burns on his cheeks. A long scar ran from his left eye to his ear. He had short black hair and glittering black eyes.

He stood on the veranda and shouted. Batsheva went out and indicated the garden and the orchard with her hand. He nodded his head, put the hoe down, and began to take off his clothes. Batsheva turned pale and he looked at her with a silly grin. Two rows of teeth gleamed at her. She ran into the house and went straight to the window overlooking the garden. From outside the house looked dark. The gardener could not see her in the window. He undressed down to his swollen underpants. Riva came to stand beside her and looked wordlessly outside. He took up the hoe and started slowly chopping. From the window his dark slender body shone with perspiration. With every rise and fall of the hoe, the muscles of his arms and stomach tensed and relaxed, his hairy armpits were covered and exposed, and his slender legs straightened and bent.

Riva gasped for breath and her hands began to sweat. Her bosom rose and fell. Batsheva turned to look at her. Suddenly she said, "Look at him, Riva. It can drive you out of your mind, can't it?"

Riva looked at her in disgust.

"You're a whore," she hissed. "I've always known it."

Riva did not take her eyes off the naked youth in the garden.

"Go away!" shrieked Batsheva. "Go away and leave me alone. I'm asking you, Riva, can't you hear me? I want to be alone for once!"

Riva retired in alarm to their room.

Batsheva went out onto the veranda and called the youth. He was embarrassed and looked shyly at his swollen underpants.

"Come here, water, water!" cried Batsheva.

He shook his head.

"Come here, come here," cried Batsheva. "Don't be afraid."

She took him into the house, and when she opened the door of their room she found Riva lying convulsed and breathless on the bed.

"Get out please!" commanded Batsheva, and Riva saw the Arab boy standing next to her sister in his underpants, rolling his eyes.

"There are other rooms, why must it be here, on father's bed?" gasped Riva.

"That's the way I want it," said Batsheva.

Riva got up and Batsheva helped her out of the room. In the living room Riva fell onto an armchair and imagined that she was dying. Her vision was blurred. She stopped her ears, but the high-pitched whine went on and on inside her head. Later her breathing became regular again, and she did not know how much time had passed or what had happened in the meantime. She felt better, and the old tune began playing in her head again, "I must hang on . . . I must not break . . ."

Batsheva opened the door and the youth went into the garden, looking around him with bewildered black eyes. He put on his khaki trousers and tried to sweep the hoe through the air again, but his arms seemed too feeble to lift it into the air and the blade dragged listlessly over the ground.

Batsheva came into the salon freshly bathed and smelling of almond soap, with an angelic expression on her face, serene and full of compassion. She sat down on the arm of the chair and stroked Riva's hair. She felt her sister shuddering and said, "I'm clean now, Riva. Cleaner than I was before. Cleaner than I've ever been in my life."

"I wasn't fair to you," said Riva. "I have no right to interfere in your affairs. I've never really understood you or been fair to you. I forgot that everyone doesn't live simply and solely for me but for themselves too."

"I often forget that too, Riva," sighed Batsheva. "But now I know that we two are different, and that's why we're lonely."

"Does one feel so much sorrow afterward?" smiled Riva.

"Did you have an attack?" asked Batsheva.

"Yes."

"A bad one?"

"Yes. I think I lost consciousness for a while."

"And at the same time I was . . ."

"You couldn't have helped me. I told you I'm not cross with you."

"But?"

"Nothing. I just want to be well, that's all."

"You must see a doctor," said Batsheva.

"The air here is humid and it's not good for me, I know it."

"And you think that the doctor will tell you to go and live somewhere else?"

"There's trouble in the country now and traveling is dangerous."

Batsheva bowed her head. She sat pensively on the arm of the chair and said nothing.

"The Arabs are stoning the buses and killing Jews," added Riva listlessly.

"You won't have to travel to the ends of the earth," commented Batsheva.

"I want to stay here with you."

"Silly, don't cry. You're not going to die. Soon the summer will be over. The winters are easier for you. Wait until after the holidays and we'll see."

Batsheva hugged her sister and clasped her to her bosom. Riva breathed in the bitter smell of the almond soap and the heat that rose from Batsheva's white body.

IN THE AFTERNOON the Arab boy shouted from the garden. He had finished clearing the thorns from the front garden. Batsheva instructed him to start work on the orchard, and while he was uprooting the thorns, to dig basins round the trees and pull out the couch grass.

He seemed to have recovered his strength; his face was proud and smiling. The scar under his eye trembled and shone with sweat. She smiled at him, and he made for the orchard with his head held high and a prancing step, the hoe on his shoulder.

He worked for a week, and from time to time Batsheva would call him to come and have a glass of water. Afterward he would emerge weak and bewildered as usual. At night he slept in the orchard and waited for her to come out with her flimsy nightgown fluttering round her knees.

After a week he ran away without even coming to ask for his money.

ONCE MORE THE engineer came and ordered them to leave the house. Langfuss too came several times to try to persuade them to leave, and he made them many propositions. They did not even react. The neighbors peered anxiously over the fence, afraid to say anything to them.

Riva promised the engineer that they would repair the

house. He looked at them skeptically and shrugged his shoulders. After he left the painter came. He hung a metal frame punched with holes on the front wall and began painting over it. The two sisters stood on the veranda and watched him indifferently. When he had finished painting he removed the metal frame from the wall, revealing the following announcement:

THIS HOUSE IS DANGEROUS AND UNDER ORDER OF
DEMOLITION. ANYONE RENTING OR BUYING THIS HOUSE
DOES SO AT HIS OWN RISK.

· 31 ·

WHAT HAPPENED NEXT TOOK RIVA BY SURPRISE AND BROUGHT her to the point of collapse. Batsheva got up one morning and she looked different. Riva regarded her apprehensively and tried to guess what had happened in the night. She had been sleeping next to her and had not noticed anything. Batsheva held her head high, her lids lowered in an expression of superior contempt, and her lips narrowed. Riva was alarmed. The scent of the impending storm rose in her nostrils. Batsheva did not reply to her questions. Riva went up to her sister and examined her closely, but she could not make her talk. She moved about the house silent and menacing.

Riva followed her like a shadow through all the rooms and passages into which she tried to escape. She demanded an answer to her questions; she pleaded, insisted, shouted. Batsheva stubbornly pursed her mouth and refused to even give her a hint with her eyes.

"You're trying to drive me crazy, Batsheva," said Riva. "I

know you are. Up to now you've tried everything you could without success. Now you're trying to play the great lady looking down on her wretched servant. You're right, we were always your servants. We danced attendance on you. We were thirsty for every smile of thanks you bestowed on us. And why? Why didn't you ever do a thing for yourself in your life? Why didn't you cook, wash, clean the house, why didn't you ever help with anything? Batsheva! We were all your willing slaves, without even knowing why. Father, Mother, Chasida, me, and the whole world! What gives you the right to put on airs? What gives you the right not to talk to me?"

A passion of speech took hold of Riva. There had been days when the sisters hardly spoke to each other. But now that Batsheva was as silent as a blank, hostile wall, Riva could not stop talking. She knew that she would regret it and be ashamed of herself later, but a force beyond her comprehension compelled her to go on. Batsheva leaned against the cupboard in the living room with her hands hanging by her sides in disdainful resignation, and Riva grabbed her by the sleeve to force her to open her mouth. Batsheva recoiled in disgust.

Riva tried to cry, but she could not. She rubbed her eyes and twisted her lips, and Batsheva favored her with a thin smile at the corners of her lips.

"You're getting old, Batsheva," said Riva in a stern voice. "It's obvious in your behavior and your face. The suffering of us all is engraved on your brow. What you did to Mother, to Father, to Chasida, to me. Everything you did to us. You ruined our lives. You put thoughts in our heads that would never have occurred to us, in order to drive us crazy. Everyone wonders what it is that's eating you up, where you get so much venom to torment us."

Batsheva did not reply. Small and thin, she stood in the corner of the room in a defensive posture, as if she were afraid that Riva was about to attack her physically. Riva hoped that Batsheva would break down and she would gain the upper hand. She was breathing normally and her heartbeat was regular, but nevertheless she dropped onto a chair and began to gasp for breath. She closed her eyes and laid her hand on her heart. Batsheva tiptoed out of the room.

Riva rose and followed her. Batsheva shut herself up in the bedroom. "If it wasn't for you," Riva screamed and pounded on the door with her fists, "if it wasn't for you we would all be alive and happy. I would have been a wife and mother years ago! Batsheva! Take pity on us all, on the dead and the living, and go away. Go away and leave us alone!"

Batsheva did not reply. Riva went to the kitchen and fetched the rolling pin. She began beating violently on the door. Batsheva did not react. A crack appeared in the door next to the lock, and Riva began to bang on the hinges to loosen them.

Slowly the door opened and Batsheva peeped out with an expression of alarm on her face. Riva raised the rolling pin to bring it down on her sister's head, but suddenly the expression on Batsheva's face changed to one of calm disdain, and Riva turned to stone. Batsheva smiled bitterly, but she did not open her mouth. Riva dropped her hands and the rolling pin fell to the floor. Batsheva bent down slowly and picked it up. Helpless rage and fury blazed in Riva's eyes at the sight of her sister's coldness.

"Batsheva! You bitch!" she screamed. Batsheva glanced apprehensively in the direction of the neighbors' houses. "Go away, Batsheva, go away! Leave us alone! Go to hell and don't ever come back! Not ever!"

The neighbors peered out of their windows. Riva was hysterical. Batsheva took her gently by the arm and led her into one of the empty rooms at the back of the house. Riva did not resist. She sat down on a chair, but she kept on screaming.

Batsheva remembered what her father had once done in similar circumstances. Her eyes glinted with determination, but her hand rebelled. Riva screamed again. Her face was red as fire and her hair was standing on end. Suddenly hard, desperate blows landed on her face, one after the other, first on her left cheek, then on her right, until she fell silent with the shock, her face white and rigid, only her ears still flaming. Red fingermarks appeared on both her cheeks like scars.

"Murderess," she muttered. "You're a murderess. You drove me out of my mind. That's what you wanted. That's what I've been afraid of all my life. Murderess."

Batsheva looked at her without a word.

"Speak to me," pleaded Riva. "Say something to me, Batsheva. Now that you've murdered me, speak to me."

Riva sobbed quietly. She got up, exhausted, and tried to lean her head on Batsheva's shoulder. Batsheva did not try to stop her, but she did not embrace her as usual and she did not say a word. She stood like stone and waited for Riva to desist.

But Riva did not desist. She was prepared to stand like that until Batsheva was reconciled with her. When Batsheva wearied of standing with her sister's head on her shoulder, she led her into the living room, sat her down on the sofa, and went to her room. Riva relaxed a little and breathed heavily. Her heart pounded and her whole body shook. She lay down, bathed in perspiration. She remembered Chasida and began weeping again, gasping for breath. When she opened her eyes Batsheva was standing in the door with a glass of water in her hand.

Like a ministering angel, like a sister of mercy. A pure, mute smile on her thin lips. Her pale, dazzling eyes shaded by her lashes. Her two hands outstretched with the glass of water. Riva was afraid that her eyes were deceiving her. Batsheva stood like a statue, waiting for Riva to get up and take the glass. Riva did not get up. She stared at her reproachfully, expectantly. Finally she took the glass and sipped the water slowly. Batsheva went on standing there and looking at her.

"You poisoned us all," Riva said. "Where do you get all that poison from?"

BATSHEVA'S SILENCE LASTED for about a week. Riva recovered and made up her mind that she would never reveal her suffering again. She went on with her work as if nothing had happened. Only the shame went on scalding her heart. How she had humiliated herself in front of her sister! They went on sleeping together, out of habit, despite the barrier between them. One morning Riva got up and got dressed. She always got up before Batsheva. But Batsheva was awake; she lay looking at her sister. Behind her back Riva suddenly heard, "Riva!"

A shudder ran down her spine. The voice was familiar and yet terrible in its newness. Like a voice from the dead. Riva did not turn her face. Her hands shook and began to sweat.

"Riva, I think I'm pregnant."

Riva turned around. Batsheva looked at her as usual, calm and indifferent.

"Don't look at me like that," Riva said. "Why have you decided to speak to me?"

"Why not?" asked Batsheva.

"Why haven't you spoken to me all this time?"

"I wanted to be alone a little."

"You have no right to be alone here. I live here too."

"There's enough room in this house for each of us to be alone."

"Are you trying to drive me out of my mind again?"

"Why?"

"What's all this about being pregnant?"

"I only said I thought I was. It's not certain."

"I'm sure that it's not certain."

"Don't be so sure," said Batsheva mysteriously.

AFTER A TIME Batsheva acknowledged her mistake. "You can never tell," she said. "We're only flesh and blood."

Riva agreed with her.

· 32 ·

RIVA'S HEALTH WORSENED. THE ATTACKS GREW FREQUENT AND regular. In the end they plucked up courage and went to the doctor.

It was the first time Batsheva had gone out into the street. She seemed very pale against the background of the street, and Riva looked at her curiously to see how she would react to this meeting with the colony. Batsheva was as cool as usual, but a flicker of terror flashed through her eyes every time anyone walked past them.

She hardly recognized the street. Many old houses had been torn down and big new ones had gone up in their place. The gardens in Founders Street had shrunk and apartment blocks had risen on every side.

When they emerged from the doctor's office, Riva's face was downcast and her eyes were wet.

"But you knew yourself, Riva, that you would have to go away."

"It doesn't make any difference."

They went home and their hearts were heavy. They had no appetite. Their desolation grew.

"Couldn't I stay until the winter at least?"

"In this damp? Out of the question."

"It's hard to leave like this."

"With leaking walls, with the danger of the house collapsing on top of us? Riva, for both our sakes, you must look after your health. Do you remember what we used to talk about during the winter nights?"

"In winter I feel better," said Riva.

"Do as you please. Afterward you'll say that I made you leave so that I would inherit the house."

"The house?" scoffed Riva, pointing to the crumbling walls.

Batsheva uttered a heartfelt sigh, placed two fingers on her temples, and closed her eyes.

"It's the end of summer, Batsheva," said Riva. "Can you feel the wind coming from the south?"

"What south? There's no window facing south here at all," said Batsheva.

WHEN AUTUMN CAME Riva had a severe attack. Her face swelled up and her breath rattled. The doctor recommended a sanitarium and Riva gave in.

In the morning they got onto the bus with two large suitcases in their hands. In the bus they sat and looked out of the windows. Riva tried not to cry. There were two new lines on Batsheva's forehead and at the corners of her mouth, lines of bitterness. Batsheva's getting old, thought Riva. Before evening they arrived at the sanitarium in the hills. The view did not capture Riva's heart. These were not the hills she had seen in her imagination.

But she submitted to her fate, and when she saw the people sitting in the sanitarium gardens she smiled sadly. "Everyone here is old."

Batsheva clasped her to her bosom. "It's only for a little while, Riva. Until you get better."

Riva was given a white room, gleaming with cleanliness and smelling of disinfectant. Batsheva stayed with her for a few days. The first night neither of them could sleep, because of the smell of the disinfectant, and the next day they were tired and had no appetite. After a few days Riva was reconciled. It seemed to her that her health was improving. She told Batsheva that she could go home. "We mustn't leave the house empty," she said. "The municipality might take advantage of our absence to tear it down."

The next morning they parted without tears. Riva promised to get better quickly and come home.

When Batsheva got onto the bus and left the sanitarium, a string seemed to snap in her heart. The bus jolted her body over the dirt road but her soul was empty. Every minute she expected Arabs to stone the bus and murder its passengers. Like they did to Baruch.

The road was bright and empty. Slowly she recovered her spirits. The vision of the sanitarium and of Riva walking alone in the gardens faded from her eyes, and the memory of her big house in the colony strengthened her a little.

She would get little Napoleon to mend the cracks. She would ask the engineer to draw up a plan for strengthening the foundations. She would retile the floors, whitewash the walls like in the sanitarium, white both inside and out.

Suddenly the driver woke her up. The bus was standing in the colony. He stood at her head, smiling. The bus was empty.

"I'm growing old," thought Batsheva.

She walked up Founders Street with her heart pounding. At the gate she paused and looked at her house, at the neat, clean yard. She opened the iron gate and without closing it behind her walked slowly up the path, as if she were walking in a dream. She opened the front door and stood there in a daze.

The house was dark and empty. She hurried to her room. The windows were shuttered and the smell of the bedclothes lay heavily in the stuffy room. She flung herself onto the bed and hugged the pillow and wept. Finally she got up and went into the kitchen to have something to eat. She was hungry and she ate heartily. She felt intoxicated. She opened all the shutters and the windows wide.

Evening came early, and since she was very tired she went straight to bed. She lay alone; every rustle outside froze her blood. She got up and went into the living room and poured herself a glass of brandy. She took a deep breath and felt better.

Her father rose above the foot of her bed and turned his face to the wall. His face was full of spittle. The big clock in the passage struck the hour, and everything went dark. The room was silent, listening to the night, and her father was no longer there. She stood up and took a blanket and tried to fall asleep. She lay open eyed. She switched on the light and started walking around the house, opening the doors of all the rooms, switching on the lights, and then switching them off again and closing the doors. She went back to her room and tried to read. She read for hours without knowing what she was reading.

She switched off the light and pulled the blanket up to her ears. Chasida stood muttering next to her bed. Her little amber earrings shone with a dull, flickering light. Suddenly Chasida took off her wig and her shaven head rose above her shoulders like the stump of a tree.

Batsheva knew that it was an illusion. She tried to scream and she couldn't. She tried to touch the apparition but she couldn't move. Outside a crowd of people were collecting and shouting rhythmically as if they were chanting slogans.

She woke up and found herself in the empty room. She hurried to the window but was unable to see anything. She wrapped herself in a bathrobe and cautiously opened the door. Throngs of people were celebrating in the street, shouting and cheering.

A stab of insult cleaved her body and her self-hate grew intense. She tried to decipher the rhythmic cries without success. She heard only their lethal rhythm, advancing like a flood. There were lights on in the neighbors' houses, but she could not see anyone inside them.

Now she heard voices rising in song, the songs she used to hear when there was dancing at the cultural committee. Her hand gripped one of the bars of the gate which rose above its fellows like a polished bayonet. Her fingers closed hard around the bar, to bend or break it.

· 33 ·

THE TEACHER BOROCHOV AND HADASSAH SAT AT HOME. THE little girl had woken up while they were out and started to cry. Hadassah went to her and began telling her about the celebrations outside. Borochov was not affected by the general glee. But he made an effort to look happy and smile at his friends kissing each other in the street and announcing that they were going to dance till dawn.

The voices from outside continued to invade the house. Suddenly calm descended on Borochov. It seemed to him that the poem he wanted to write was trembling at his fingertips.

He sat down immediately at his desk. He tried to write a title. But then he decided to put off writing the title until the poem itself was finished. He held his pen over the sheet of paper, closed his eyes, and waited for the moment of grace to come and bring the lines pouring out of his pen. Suddenly he suspected that this time too he would write nothing and he was overcome with rage.

Hadassah came into the room and he knew that he would have to put his pen down and that would be that. She sat down behind him; her eyes bored into his neck and paralyzed his hands.

"Yedidya," she said.

"Yes, Hadassah."

"The child is asleep."

He said nothing.

"I'm going to bed now. Goodnight."

"Goodnight, Hadassah."

"The nights are getting chilly. Don't forget to cover yourself."

"I'll be joining you in a minute."

"It doesn't matter," said Hadassah, and went out of the room.

The voices coming from outside pounded in his ears and confused his thoughts. He went to close the window and the scent of the jasmine flooded his face. Hadassah's jasmine. The room was still. On the desk the paper and pen waited. He sat down and leaned his forehead against his cold hand.

He knew now that he would never write the poem. He stood up again and went over to the closed window. He pressed his nose against the cold windowpane. He could see only his nose squashed against the glass and the room reflected in the windowpane, the desk, the chairs, the paper.

The summer was over and the winter had not yet begun. The trees in Nechama's yard had already shed their guavas, whose smell was the smell of autumn. The roads were full of dust, and in the citrus groves the fruit was ready for picking. But the rain would only come after the holidays. It would drip from the roofs of the houses, wash the windows and the old cypresses next to the fences, collect in puddles at the sides of the roads. And at night it would gurgle in the gutters and disturb his sleep.